# *Belle Isle*

# **Rodney Lockwood**

ABOUT THE COVERS

The front cover is a morning view of Belle Isle following its transformation from an uninhabited island in the Detroit River to a magnet for capital, a dynamic new community founded on the principles of freedom and opportunity.

The back cover shows a typical evening street scene in the downtown area of Belle Isle, a vibrant walking community.

The covers show what can happen in Belle Isle, and in the process transform Detroit into a dynamic city of its own, replacing destitution and dole with dignity and jobs. Let freedom ring.

# TABLE OF CONTENTS

# Introduction

Detroit needs a game changer. This book uses Belle Isle to provide that change.

In 1950, Detroit was a vibrant city, the wealthiest in the nation. Today, the city has lost most of its population and wealth. Many good people have worked hard to improve Detroit and their progress should be recognized. But Detroit continues to have financial issues without a solution on the horizon, and it may have passed the point of offering real hope for her struggling people. The continuation of the government dole by itself, which hasn't succeeded over the years, isn't the answer. A new idea is needed, a dramatic act which has the power to turn all this around. This book is about that dramatic act, Detroit's game changer.

The setting is Belle Isle, 30 years in the future. It is fiction, but the main characters are real people, whose names have been changed to protect their identities. Darin is one of the most creative people I know. He has the rare combination of a keen sense of aesthetics coupled with a fiery passion for individual liberty and freedom. I can see him pulling this off. His dear friend Joe will make his mark in the world too, but in this book it is in another country.

Belle Isle is an island in the Detroit River, owned by the City of Detroit. It is uninhabited and shares Detroit's disrepair. Yet, for all the current squalor, it may be the most important 982 acres in the state of Michigan, perhaps in the entire country. What Darin does with Belle isle is remarkable in itself, but even more important,

Belle Isle can turn around Detroit and beyond. Belle Isle's culture of unlimited opportunity fueled by a culture of "can do" optimism will create a firestorm of jobs and wealth creation. The sparks will jump the river and start similar fires in Detroit and Southeast Michigan. The light from those fires may even show the way for our country to once again find the power of freedom on which it was founded.

This book is not about creating an island of wealth, even though it does. Of course it will attract wealth and wealth is fine, but what will distinguish it from other city-states or small countries is its spirit and optimism. Even the less wealthy will bask in the sunshine of freedom and be lifted by its opportunity. Unfettered from too many rules and regulations, from taxing the wrong things, from inefficient self-serving government, Belle Isle will become the "Midwest Tiger," rivaling Singapore and Hong Kong in its economic miracle.

As a lover of liberty and a believer in the human fabric, I have over my years observed a slow crawl toward the lowest common denominator. Not that society here in the U.S. used to be perfect, but there are many tangible examples of a deterioration of the quality of life, even as the standard measures of material wealth have greatly increased. Over the last 60 years, the inflation adjusted Gross Domestic Product per capita increased more than three fold. That is good. The opportunities for women and minorities have greatly increased. That is good. But think of all the behaviors and norms that exist today, which in many cases did not 60 years ago. We fear for our safety and many of us don't venture into Detroit. Concealed weapon permits are considered and often obtained. We blame others for our mistakes and poor judgment. If we slip and fall for most any reason, our first thought is not how careless we were, but whether we should call an attorney. We buy lottery tickets with our hard earned money to give us some hope, even though we know the "average return" is at best 50%. We don't trust or believe in our government, particularly Washington, to do the right thing. We believe Washington answers to special interests, which exact favors from elected officials in exchange for funding their re-election campaigns.

This book is about fixing that — about creating a social laboratory which takes new approaches in the areas of government services, taxation, labor, money and legal systems, among others. To give credit, many of the ideas are not mine; they are ones I have heard about over the years that have stuck with me as making sense. I hope the reader understands I am not seeking to claim them as my own. I simply subscribe to the notion that true power arises from meaning, meaning that uplifts and enables. Witness the fact that Mahatma Gandhi brought down British Colonialism without raising his hand in anger. Rather, it was the power of selflessness, faith in the intrinsic dignity of man and our divinely acquired right to freedom, sovereignty and self-determination. And so this shall be the power that gives rise to the miracle of Belle Isle.

So dear reader, I hope you enjoy your journey in the future and join me in imagining how the shining light of Belle Isle can save Detroit and show the way for the United States as well.

# Commentary

By:    Hal Sperlich

Former President, Chrysler Corporation

Member of the Automotive Hall of Fame

Patriot

When I was given the opportunity to read *Belle Isle*, I couldn't put it down.  It was two hours of reading with amazement that someone could visualize a solution to one of America's most enduring human tragedies, and that the solution would be based on the same principles on which our nation was founded...........freedom, opportunity and the self-reliance of the people.  That's big.

I have no doubt that Belle Isle could become the economic miracle Rod Lockwood has envisioned.  The dynamism and success of any society reflect its fundamental principles.  In Belle Isle's case, individual freedom and self-reliance, along with a government that exists primarily to facilitate these values, provide the context within which men and women can reach the upper limits of their potential.

Just eighty years ago, the cost of government in America was 13% of GDP.  Today, ever expanding government consumes about 40% of total GDP.  Much of these shockingly high costs are imbedded in the costs of American made products and services through taxation, or borrowed, seriously reducing our competiveness today and making it even tougher on future generations.

Belle Isle, with government spending as a percentage of GDP less than half the U.S. rate, would need no taxes on income, capital gains, dividends, interest or estates. As such it would be a magnet for capital and would be the most attractive place to work or do business in the world. Thus the economic miracle would be, as they say, a slam dunk. When asked whether all this could really happen, I have to answer, I really can't see how it could fail.

Important as Belle Isle is, and as remarkable and refreshing as this miracle would be, the even bigger story may be how the power of freedom and opportunity would finally lift the long suffering people of Detroit, and provide something nothing else has yet delivered......their first real shot at the American Dream.

The billion dollars paid for the island by the original private investment group would remove the blight, reconfigure the city into smaller population centers, and provide the crucial training of the population for the work that Belle Isle's magic would bring. Belle Isle's infrastructure including its monorail system would be built for about $4 billion, funded by the citizenship payments of its original settlers. Additionally, the even greater billions of private capital that would be attracted by Belle Isle's economic advantages would create hotels, office buildings, new businesses, residences, and recreational, entertainment, and educational facilities for the people.

A new user-funded monorail would connect Belle Isle's citizens to the cultural and entertainment opportunities of a recharged downtown Detroit. On the Detroit side of the Belle Isle bridge would be everything a new community of 35,000 freedom advocates might want, from an airport to major shopping and dining facilities, major recreational facilities, a large industrial complex supporting Belle Isle businesses, and housing for the tens of thousands who would make their homes in the middle of this explosion of new activity.

All these billions of private investment, without a penny of taxpayer money, would launch a construction boom of enormous size and duration, which along with the ongoing economic activity, would provide jobs and hope for the people of Detroit.

People will move here from all over the world, bringing their capital, and even those coming without capital will do so just to see how capitalism is really supposed to work......and to see how it can replace destitution and the dole with dignity and jobs.

Would Detroiters go for this? If there are leaders of vision here, and we believe there are, they will see it as the answer to their prayers.

Nationally, there will be the usual cries that Belle Isle would provide just one more advantage for the wealthy. But as Americans begin to realize how Belle Isle could transform the lives of so many in all walks of life, they will come to understand that they will be witnessing the power of freedom in action for the benefit of all.

But would the folks in Washington go along? The typical first reaction is probably not. Too big an idea.

But then, big problems need big ideas, as well as men and women of great courage. Hopefully, there are a few of those still around.

In the end, one has to wonder how Washington could say no. How could they ignore the pleas of this long suffering people, asking only for permission to save themselves?

And finally, might this great social and economic experiment provide inspiration to our nation which has strayed so far from the path of freedom and self-reliance laid out for us by our founding fathers?

It's an enormously interesting possibility.

# CHAPTER 1

*Excellence is the result of caring more than others think is wise; risking more than others think is safe; dreaming more than others think is practical; and expecting more than others think is possible.*

*-Unknown*

## JOE'S ARRIVAL

The late afternoon sun made it difficult for Joe to recognize all the old landmarks.

Putting his sunglasses on helped, and the Renaissance Center came into view as the shuttle helicopter moved eastward north of the Detroit River toward its destination.

*Man, how different Detroit looks.*

Mini-cities surrounded by large areas of parks and farmland had replaced the sprawling neighborhoods he remembered from his youth. Joe had read about Detroit and how it had been transformed from a single large city of decay to a collection of smaller cities, each with their own identity. Even the names were different. He couldn't remember them all, only Indian Village, Eastside Village, Corktown and Palmer Woods. There were others, perhaps Darin would know.

It had been 25 years since Joe had been to Detroit. After graduating from Michigan State and going to the University of San Francisco Medical School, his life had taken a left turn of sorts.

Damascus Medical Center had contacted him in his fourth year of residency. The Arab Spring had turned into Summer. The political winds in Syria had become gentle breezes and the opportunity to make a difference in the land of his ancestors was a compelling siren song. Serving first as Deputy Director of the Cardiology Department, Joe was later promoted to the Director of the entire department. For the last five years, Joe had been Director of the Medical Center itself.

His rise through the ranks had been based on his technical competence as a surgeon and his easy way with his coworkers. People liked Joe.

He was born and raised in Michigan by his Syrian parents and his given name was Yousef Sharif, but Yousef, being Arabic for Joseph, quickly became Joe. He was tall, over 6'- 2", athletic build with blond hair and blue eyes. Women thought he was gorgeous and men were immediately put at ease by his friendly nature.

Life had slowed down a bit from the years of 80-hour work weeks. He had trained his staff well and his number two guy (who was actually a woman) kept the Medical Center running just as well, perhaps even better, than when Joe was there. Now, at 49, he was able to take some time off.

Darin and Joe had kept in touch, although he hadn't seen his old high school buddy since Joe had gone off to Syria. They followed each other's careers with great interest.

Darin attended the University of Michigan and graduated with a degree in Architecture, then got his Master in Urban Design from the University of Michigan. Darin was the most creative person Joe had ever met, excelling in art and music in his youth. Darin had an eye for shape and color that could quickly size up what looked good. Joe chuckled remembering that in high school, some of the girls would take Darin shopping with them as their fashion consultant when buying clothes.

After getting his Master, Darin worked for an international urban design firm that was affiliated with the Universiti Teknologi Malaysia. Their assignment was to plan the expansion of a part of the government sponsored city-state of Malacca in Malaysia. Malacca had been granted independence from Malaysia and had international funding, primarily from Singapore, to reconstruct a model city.

As a junior project manager, Darin studied under Savas Erdogan, the great Turkish planner. The two worked well together and melded the disciplines of urban planning and governance, achieving worldwide recognition as Malacca started its growth into the megalopolis it is today.

But Darin had his own siren song. At 29, a group of investors had contacted him and offered Darin a position to head up the planning and development of Belle Isle, an island in the Detroit River, purchased from the City of Detroit.

Every year of their separation, Darin invited Joe to come back and visit. Joe got long emails from Darin pleading for him to check out the transformation of Belle Isle from a largely abandoned park to a thriving metropolis. Joe inevitably responded he was just too busy with his Damascus duties; perhaps next year.

But a Time magazine article pushed him over the edge and now 20 some years later, Joe came home to reunite with his friend and see for himself what Darin had accomplished.

The helicopter made a right turn to the south and Belle Isle came into view. Once a largely abandoned city park, it was now teeming with buildings of all shapes and sizes, brick-lain streets interspersed with parks and green spaces. The tallest building was the 57-story Four Seasons hotel and the helicopter aimed for the hotel's helipad.

As the rotor blades wound down, Joe let the other shuttle passengers disembark first. They seemed in a hurry and he was not. There were three young, well dressed men in business suits, all carrying satchels and an attractive middle-aged woman who appeared to be Middle Eastern. Tired from the long trip from Damascus to New York and then on to Detroit, Joe was exhausted. Porters unloaded the helicopter in the afternoon breeze, dressed in black suits with white shirts. One hefted Joe's black leather suitcase onto a cart emblazoned with the Four Seasons logo, which was Joe's signal it was time to step outside. A warm July breeze greeted him.

Darin hadn't changed much. Tall and thin, but muscular with dark brown hair, Darin stood waiting near the small roof pad terminal. He was dressed in a light blue Polo shirt and beige slacks, wearing classic Ray-Ban sunglasses. He looked like his picture in the Time magazine article. Imbedded in the piece was a shot of Darin standing on the Four Seasons roof facing the camera, with Belle Isle in the background. The caption on the photo was "Nation Builder." Joe thought it was a bit much but Time always exaggerated everything — it was good for business.

They embraced and sized each other up. Almost three decades had added maturity to both but not robbed them of their youthful good looks.

"Joe, man you look great. Not changed a bit."

"Darin, you too; I think growing older agrees with you. Where's the grey hair?"

"None yet. Maybe someday. I'm still trying to eat healthy and do the right things to keep in shape. Also, we do a lot of walking here, which helps."

Inside the helipad terminal, Joe's suitcase and the porter who grabbed it had already disappeared. Darin saw Joe's concerned look and said, "Joe, you're already checked in and here's your key to the Von Mises Suite. It's on the 55th floor and has a great view. I think you'll find it comfortable. Your bag is on its way to your room. Say, you must be exhausted. Would you like to relax in your room a bit or have a drink in the bar first?"

"Darin, are you buying?" Joe smiled. Their long separation hadn't robbed them of their natural ease with one another.

The Skyline Bar was on the 56$^{th}$ floor of the hotel. It spanned the entire east end of the floor and commanded three views. To the north was Detroit; to the south Windsor; and to the east was most of Belle Isle and the Detroit River, which stretched on to its mouth at Lake St. Clair.

The hostess seated them at a plush sectional sofa facing the window with the east view of Belle Isle. The fabric color was a meld of greens and red wine, which complemented well with the verde marble cocktail table. The outside walls were comprised almost entirely of glass, which started just above the floor and rose to a point about 18 inches below the 10 foot ceiling. Cherry beams divided the ceiling into four-foot squares of stucco finished with a faint beige wash. The glass wall was interrupted every eight feet by a wood column, in the same finish as the ceiling beams. The west wall was dominated by a large fireplace, trimmed with a marble surround and hearth. The west wall was entirely cherry, with various panel molding accents. Over the fireplace was a painting of a sailboat regatta. It appeared to Joe each seating area was individually done. The look was both elegant and cozy.

The hostess summoned the waiter.

"Mr. Fraser, the usual sir?"

"Come on Michael, what's this Mr. Fraser stuff?" Darin turned to Joe. Pointing to Michael, he said, "I've known this guy for at least 10 years. He used to work at the Book Cadillac hotel in Detroit. I almost begged him to come work on Belle Isle about five years ago. He's served me more drinks than I can count and now he pulls the formal thing on me. What, do you think I need to impress my friend here? Michael, meet Joe Sharif. He has come all the way from Damascus to see us. Joe is an old friend and interested in seeing what Belle Isle is all about."

Michael responded, "Thank you for the clarification, O' Mighty Exalted Maker of the Universe. The usual?"

"Michael, no, it's a little early for that. I'll take an iced tea with lemon."

"Of course. Mr. Sharif, you have come quite a long way sir, may I interest you in a glass of wine or something stronger perhaps?"

Joe, being Muslim, didn't drink and ordered iced tea, too.

The teas arrived with some raspberry scones, not ordered, but much appreciated. Over the drinks, the two friends caught up on the essentials of family, friends and work. Darin outlined the agenda for Joe.

"I have dinner reservations for us tonight at 7. That gives you about 2 ½ hours to rest and clean up. Meet me in the lobby of the hotel about 6:45 and we'll go from there. I have scheduled the days ahead starting at mid-morning. That leaves your early mornings free to communicate with Damascus before they close down. I think it's a seven-hour time difference so you should have some good overlap for taking care of business back home. Your suite has full communications including video-feed so you shouldn't miss too many beats. Today we relax and tomorrow we'll start the tour. I can't tell you how excited I am to show you everything we've done here. I think you'll find it very, very interesting."

"Darin, I really appreciate you taking time out to show me around. You must have better things to do than be my host."

"You bet I do! No seriously, when my best friend whom I haven't seen in years comes back to see me, it's a big deal. We have a lot of catching up to do. And here is my life's work and I can't wait to show you Belle Isle. There is an energy level here that I have never seen in any other part of the world. You might call it a 'can do' attitude. You will meet many fine people. And the citizens of Belle Isle are anxious to meet you. Our Belle Isle Blog, the most active we have, has run a few pieces on your visit for the past week so don't be surprised if you are recognized on the street."

## CHAPTER 2

*Freedom is never more than one generation away from extinction – it must be fought for, protected, and handed on for our children to do the same, or one day we will spend our sunset years telling our children and our children's children what it was once like in the United States when men were free.*

*-Ronald Reagan*


## THE FOUR SEASONS


The Von Mises suite was one floor below the Skyline Bar. Entering through a marble foyer, the room opened up into a tastefully decorated living room with a fireplace and large TV alcove, couch and leather chairs. Adjacent was a full kitchen with a bar. Off the living room was an office with state-of-the-art electronics including a 3-D video conference screen. Two queen size beds, chairs and ottomans filled the bedroom. Off the bedroom and wrapping around to the living room was a balcony with seating for four around a bronze and glass table. Joe estimated one could entertain about 12-15 people comfortably. He wondered who Von Mises was; he would be sure to ask Darin.


The suite had two views. To the east was Belle Isle, and beyond the Detroit River was Lake St. Clair. A sailboat regatta was underway on the lake and most of the boats had their colorful spinnakers up. A few power boats were motoring by and in the distant horizon, Joe could see a giant iron ore carrier making its way westbound in the ship channel.

To the north, Joe saw a monorail spanning across the river toward an airport on the Detroit side. It appeared to have a single runway aligned with the river, a control tower and rows of hangars on the north side. Corporate jets dotted the parking apron and a large auto parking structure occupied the southwest corner. The monorail disappeared into the parking structure on its west side, but the rail line re-emerged from the east side and connected to what appeared to be the aviation terminal in front of the airplane filled ramp. Joe didn't remember an airport near Belle Isle from his youth; it must be new.

Joe's two-hour slumber was interrupted by the hotel's front desk call. He quickly showered and dressed in black slacks and a white linen short sleeved shirt and slipped on casual leather walking shoes. Darin said to keep it comfortable.

He was waiting in the lobby as Joe stepped off the elevator. The lobby of the Belle Isle Four Seasons was both modern and timeless. Marble columns matched the marble floor and gave it a feel similar to the best hotels in Europe. The bar of the lobby was full with men and women of all ages engaged in deep conversation. Off the bar was an outdoor seating area that overlooked the river with a view to Canada. A large yacht with a Bahamian flag motored lazily upstream, its aft deck filled with couples gawking at the island, with the hotel's patio guests returning polite stares. A whooshing sound overhead brought Joe's attention to the monorail, which was a good 25 feet above the lobby floor and just gliding to a stop. An escalator ran from the lobby floor up to the monorail's loading platform.

Darin noticed Joe's gaze. "Don't worry. We won't make that one but another will be by in about two minutes. We'll catch the next one."

# CHAPTER 3

*The American Republic will endure until the day Congress discovers it can bribe the public with the public's money.*

-Alexis de Tocqueville


## MONORAIL


As they waited for the next monorail, Darin explained the transportation system.


"We have two rails. One is local and the other goes to the Transportation Center, which is off-island. The local runs counter-clockwise within the island and has 10 stops. There are five cars running the route. To do an entire loop with the stops takes about 13 minutes, so the average transit time is about half that, of course depending on where you are going. The stops include the residential districts, of which there are three; the Restaurant/Entertainment areas — two there; we also have one stop at the Financial District; one at the Market District; one at the Shopping District; one at the Sports Complex; and one at the School/Worship District.


"What we call the Transportation Shuttle has five stops on the island and then runs to the Transportation Center. That loop takes 14 minutes to do a round trip, but the longest ride would be no more than 10 minutes to get to the Transportation Center. It omits one of the Restaurant/Entertainment districts, the Market, Shopping, Sports, and School/Worship Districts. Now if you want to get from one of those to the Transportation Center, you take the local to the next Transportation served terminal and switch shuttles."

Their shuttle appeared and the two stepped through the doors. The car was half filled with people, most either talking among themselves or working their PDA's.

Darin and Joe didn't bother to take a seat for the minute or so ride to the next stop. Besides, by standing, they could take in the view of the river on one side and the busy street filled with dinner hour walkers on the other.

Joe commented on the view and Darin replied, "Yes, that is one of the reasons we went with an elevated monorail rather than a subway. Everything we do here has an aesthetic consideration and of course views are paramount. We spent hours upon hours doing computer mock-ups of what the monorail rider would see on the ride. Both the route and the building design were based on making it really interesting and beautiful to the eye. If you think about it, the monorail offers the highest amount of aesthetics in the shortest time, more than any other experience on the island. Walking views are important too of course. But when residents bring guests here, they often take the monorail around a few times as sort of a tour! The other consideration was cost feasibility. A subway system would have been more expensive and the soil conditions and de-watering issues would have been costly."

# CHAPTER 4

*The smallest minority on earth is the individual. Those who deny individual rights cannot claim to be defenders of minorities.*

*-Ayn Rand*

## LES DELICES

Back on street, they made their way a block east to the Les Delices restaurant. It was a two story building with a façade of stone, stucco and brick. Diners were seated outside by the sidewalk and Joe also noted a second floor patio with an outdoor bar. The hostess was dressed in a black cocktail dress and appeared to be of Asian descent. She knew Darin by name and led them to a private booth in the back.

The drinks were served and Darin started his story.

"Joe, you remember my brother Andrew. Well, he owns this restaurant and should be by to say hi at some point. I told him you were coming and he wants to see you. Andrew as you may remember always had an interest in cooking and food. He watched the Food Channel for hours as a boy and became the family chef of sorts in our house. Andrew's interest was in steaks and other meats but he also started growing various tomatoes and even invented a strain that has become quite popular. You should try one of the salads or tomato dishes tonight — they are quite unique. He also started a line of salsa that is manufactured in Detroit and sold in five states. It's called Vita Salsa and is very good. It's on the menu here of course — you need to try it."

"So Andrew does all the cooking? Is this his full-time thing?"

"No, he has a five-star New York-trained chef but spends time in the kitchen overseeing the menu and dabbling at it at times himself. But most of his focus is spent on the family real estate operation that he took over from our father. It originally was only in Michigan but now has properties in the southeast U.S., U.K. and a small operation in the Republic of Georgia. It's mostly senior and health care related. The headquarters are right here on Belle Isle.

"One of the great things about this location, both for Andrew and for other business people who live here is the access to markets. Michigan used to be considered one of the 'fly-over' states; companies would headquarter on the coasts and do business on the other coast, fly over us and we were largely ignored. That has changed. We now like to call ourselves the 'fly-from' state, because by being in the middle, our travel time to all the markets is shorter. It makes our location more valuable, not less.

"For example, the family company has a senior health care facility located in Charleston, S.C., about 10 minutes from Charleston airport. The total travel time from the company office to the Charleston facility is two hours and fifteen minutes. That includes the monorail ride to the Belle Isle airport, the plane to Charleston and the car ride on the other side. Of course, that's on the company airplane. By contrast, if you were in Manhattan, the total time to Charleston would be about five hours on commercial plane out of LaGuardia or four hours by corporate jet. From Los Angeles, add three hours to those numbers. Time is money."

"Interesting, but tell me about your work here."

Darin smiled. "Where do I start?"

"How about the beginning."

## CHAPTER 5

*Much of the social history of the Western world over the
past three decades has been a history of replacing what
worked with what sounded good.*

-Thomas Sowell

## BELLE ISLE HISTORY

"Joe, you said you read the Time article so I won't spend
time on every detail. But about 28 years ago, a group of
people my father knew, a loosely knit collection of free
market and liberty folks who called themselves the Troublemakers came up with the idea of forming their own
country. I suppose it would be easy to do so by buying
some island in the Caribbean and negotiating independence, but that would be remote, both from a business
standpoint and culture too. Well back in 2000, a free
market think tank based in Michigan called the Mackinac
Center published an article titled 'For Whom the Private
'Belle' Tolls – Is It Time to Sell Belle Isle?' This article
proposed selling Belle Isle to private developers who
would build a community free from the city of Detroit's
regulations and taxes. Sort of do its own thing. The
price to buy Belle Isle in the article was $370,000,000.
The Mackinac Center author consulted with one of the
Troublemakers on the idea, so this person was very familiar with the whole concept and in fact supplied some
of the numbers with regard to valuation. The idea remained dormant for a few years, but as Detroit became
more and more destitute, losing population with huge
budget problems and in search of a solution, the idea
came back to the surface. So they offered a billion dollars for the island, a little over $1,000,000 per acre,
which in today's U.S. dollars is equivalent to $2.5 billion.
But the investor group, as part of the offer, required Belle

Isle become its own political jurisdiction, with its own laws, taxation, currency, citizenship, everything.

"Although the city badly needed the money and the offer was very lucrative, there was a lot of opposition.

"Some Detroit groups were aghast. 'How dare you take away our jewel,' they would say. There were a lot of protests. But the leaders in Detroit saw the possibilities, not only what the money would do for Detroit, which badly needed funds for neighborhood relocation, but also how the new community would be a magnet for investment in the area.

"Others labeled the idea just a tax haven — a place for rich people to hang out and avoid paying U.S. income taxes. We countered that by offering to becoming a commonwealth of the United States, similar to the status of the Northern Marianas Islands; so we weren't setting a precedent. We entered into a tax arrangement with the U.S. where Belle Isle citizens pay whatever taxes citizens of other countries who do business in the U.S. pay. No more, no less — just like the Canadians who live in Canada but do business in the U.S."

Darin continued. "Some worried if Belle Isle were allowed to form its own commonwealth, others would want to follow. For example, Texas had a secessionist group that was quite vocal. 'If Belle Isle could leave, why can't we?' But we pointed out that Texas was having huge job and population growth and was doing just fine under its statehood status, while Detroit was a mess looking for a solution. Also, we weren't leaving, just remaking ourselves.

"But the biggest group was the doubters, most who thought the idea was great but impossible to achieve. 'It can't be done.' 'You guys are crazy wackos and so forth.' But the more people talked about it, the more the vision became clear. A place where people had unlimited opportunity and freedom. Where government got out of the way. Where people were united in their common vision of opportunity, responsibility, honesty and respect for each other. It was very powerful, and it was inevitable something major was going to happen.

Then Detroit ran out of money. Some groups in Detroit put together a great plan on how to spend the billion dollars on training and consolidation of the better areas of Detroit. The fact that the Belle Isle investors were going to spend another $4 billion on infrastructure and $20 billion in private construction was going to create a ton of jobs for Detroiters. And half the capital was going to come from outside the U.S. along with 15,000 immigrants from abroad. A top economic consulting firm studied the issue and predicted that Belle Isle would be a magnet for capital from all over the world, as its 10% cost of government would make it *uber-competitive*, compared to the typical 40% of many of the western economies. It turned out to be true. So the Troublemakers became the *Troublesolvers.*

"You mentioned the Troublemakers were free market liberty types. So is this a libertarian based society?" Joe asked.

"Who can say?" Darin answered. "We really resist labels here. Back when this idea got started, the U.S. was extremely divided. Well, you know that - you were still here at that point. There were conservatives who despised the liberals as being free loaders and simply wanting to take that which they hadn't earned or deserved. The liberals hated the conservatives as being uncaring for the less fortunate and puppets of the fat cat millionaires and crony capitalists. Then you had the libertarians and Tea Party types who just wanted to be left alone and freed of intrusive government. But my point is that it is impossible to accurately label the complex views of life and society with single words. And to try to do so only introduces false perceptions of the beliefs of people. So we don't use those terms here. Of course, we have our viewpoints, but we drill down to the specifics of the issue and are always looking for solutions. If you had to label us, we might be called 'solutionists'."

Darin continued, "But being a solutionist doesn't make someone a pragmatist who sacrifices principles. Our community is built on three principles.

"The first is that our system of government is small and only performs those functions that cannot be served well by a free people in a free market. The government is also highly transparent and works hard to be free of influence and corruption.

"The second principle is our community must have exceptional aesthetics. I'm talking about our architecture and planning. Although we believe we spend our money wisely here, we don't take the cheapest way out. We believe the aesthetic environment is as important as the water and air quality.

"Third, we respect all our citizens, no matter what their station in life or our society. And we promote self-reliance, as freedom goes hand-in-hand with personal responsibility. We share a common ground here in the first two principles. We teach in our schools, voluntarily I might add, that limited government and the beauty of our surroundings are important core values which bind us, just like our English language."

"Why is English so important? Many countries have multiple languages."

"True, but we believe in understanding. Understanding others' viewpoints, wishes and desires requires a common language. We don't always agree, but we always understand."

Darin continued with his story. "Initially, Washington was opposed for the reasons I mentioned before but mostly they didn't want some tax haven that would suck revenue from the federal government, which of course seemed to have an insatiable appetite for finding money from any source.

"So, what the Troublemakers did was to offer to limit citizenship to 50,000 people, which the Feds seemed to tolerate, and frankly is all we can fit on the island. Right now we're at about 35,000. They also agreed to make an annual payment to the federal government that would cover the defense costs of Belle Isle, the assumption being our security here depends upon the U.S. military. That number is calculated based on the per capita defense budget times the number of citizens we have. We are probably paying too much as the U.S. is still embarking on foreign ventures from time to time that don't have any tangible defensive component, but we don't argue about it — we just pay it. In terms of the U.S. dollar back 28 years ago, it worked out to about $2,000 per person."


Joe interrupted, "So Darin, how do you pay that tax? Or for that matter, what is your tax system?"

## CHAPTER 6

*It is no contradiction—the most important single thing we can do to stimulate investment in today's economy is to raise consumption by major reduction of individual income tax rates.*

*-John F. Kennedy*

## TAXATION

Darin answered, "It's a broad question and one the Troublemakers spent a lot of time debating. Now understand, this was before I was recruited to work on the project, so I'm not familiar with all the ideas that were discussed, only those that survived.

"There were some broad principles that governed. First and possibly most important, taxes had to be transparent. So the European model of a Value Added Tax was quickly discarded, because it was added at different levels of production and is basically a hidden consumption tax, embedded in the price of the product.

"Second, we never tax that which we like to encourage. We want to create and have wealth, so we never tax the creation of wealth. No income tax or tax on investment, which creates wealth. So that's off the table and we never consider it. We have no tax on income, either personal or corporate. We have no inheritance tax. Death is penalty enough — there shouldn't be a tax on top of it! Now some countries, especially those that can't keep their spending under control, say we are a tax haven because we don't tax income or wealth creation, and we say if that's your definition of a tax haven, we are proud to be one."

"So you're not a tax haven?" Joe asked, clearly doubtful.

"No, we're a spending haven! Effective and efficient. Transparent and trustworthy. The taxes follow the spending and we never borrow to support our spending."

Darin continued, "We encourage user fees. So if our government provides a service that is used only by certain people or groups, we charge for it. 'You get what you pay for and you pay for what you get.' That is provided the costs of collection are fair and efficient. For example, let's say we provide a service that is rather low priced, say one Rand, but it costs us half a Rand to collect the tax for that service. We would consider that inefficient, a 50% collection cost. We also consider whether the service is widely used or not, when we decide whether to separately place a user tax or tax from the general fund.

"But before we talk about what we do tax, let's spend time on what the government of Belle Isle provides. First of all, we try to provide as little as possible. I know that sounds silly, but it really is based on the principle that the private sector inherently provides better service and a better product than does the government. That's because profit is a motivator. We love profit. If a process doesn't have profit, we look at it with deep and profound skepticism!

"But we also acknowledge that profit without competition is worse than the profitless scenario. So if for whatever reason a process will be only provided by one company in the private sector, then the government will step in and either regulate the process or take it over completely. The regulatory option is preferable to the government option of course. An example is the public power utility. We have a private company here that has built a mini nuclear reactor using nuclear submarine technology, but we don't have enough of a population base to support another reactor owned by a second company. So we regulate the rates for the power. The rates are computed by a formula based on risk-adjusted return on capital with incentives for reliability, efficiency and expense reduction. Some of our smart financial types came up with it and the private power company is fine with it and everyone is happy. We have the most reliable and lowest cost power in the area as a result. It works out very well. However, if a competitor came into the market place and built a second power plant, we would sell ours off to the private sector.

"Take for example our monorail. There's only room for one on Belle Isle and the monorail is considered like a road or sidewalk — a necessary part of our community; it is a public utility. We have a combination of base plus user fees. We take the initial capital cost of the monorail and the debt service required for the capital and that gets paid from the general fund. However, the operating expenses, payroll, electricity, maintenance, etc. are paid by user fees. Each of us has a transponder ID that is recognized every time we use the monorail, which then translates to a quarterly bill. It is very minor and amounts to a few Rand a month. Everyone uses the monorail and doesn't think twice about the cost.

"Some of our general tax revenue comes from transaction or consumption taxes. So we basically have a sales tax on goods and services. It amounts to about 10% and is collected by the seller/provider and remitted to us on a monthly basis. One of the things we like about this tax is the ease and efficiency of the collection process. We have certain exemptions, primarily on the services side, but only for efficiency of collection issues. If the time spent on the collection/remitting typically takes over 25% of the tax collected, we have a review process for exempting that activity. It makes no sense to spend a lot of time on tax collection. This is one of the lessons we learned from the U.S. government's ill-advised activities on the federal income tax. Its costs of collection and the taxpayer compliance and reporting costs were huge. I remember hearing back in 2010 Americans spent over 7.5 billion hours on tax preparation. Ninety percent of the tax returns had to be prepared by hired professionals. We didn't want to repeat that mistake.

"We don't tax sales or transfers of goods or services between companies. That would be a hidden tax and would not meet our transparency requirement. We also don't tax spending money on capital investment. So if a rich person buys a yacht for a million Rand, we would tax it at 10%, but if he built a plant making widgets for a million Rand, there would be no tax.

"One of our major sources of taxes is the property tax. But our property tax is different than the system typically used in the United States. In the U.S., the tax is a percentage of the total value of the property. So if the owner builds a structure or improves his property, then his taxes go up. We don't think that is right. What additional benefit has government given to the property owner to justify the additional tax? What additional cost has government borne as a result of the improvement? Government might argue the costs of police and fire protection have risen as the size of the building has increased, but that is a weak connection. The major increases in costs are borne by the insurance companies that insure the buildings against fire or other losses, but those costs are directly passed on to the property owner in the form of insurance premiums."

"So what is your property tax system, if not based on value?"

"We base it on the value contributed by government, not by the property owner. And that value is the land on which the building is placed, not the building itself."

Joe was perplexed, "You mean you only tax the raw land value — what the owner builds on it is untaxed?"

"Exactly. If government provides good services in the way of police and fire protection, keeps crime low, allows good schools to flourish, master plans in a rational and pleasing way, provides good transportation, promotes liberty and unlimited opportunity, is corruption free and has reasonable spending and taxes, than people will want to live here. If the demand to be here is high, prices go up and stay up. So that's the wealth government has created for the private citizen and property owner and that's what gets taxed. What the property owner does for himself by building from scratch or constructing an improvement, that is not taxed."

Joe was scratching his head as he mulled over what Darin had said. It just seemed to make too much sense.

"But how do you determine what the land value is and split that off? In the typical system, when a property sells, don't you have hard evidence of the total value, but not of the portions attributed to the land and to the buildings?"

"Good question. In the old tax system, the assessor would value a property based on its recent sales price, or in the case where that particular piece had not sold recently, then comparable properties are used to estimate value. So the vast majority of properties are taxed on estimates of value, not on actual numbers. My point here is even the old system, supposedly based on hard numbers, is far from perfect, but is based on a rough estimation. So we are not expecting perfection in our system either, just striving for more equity.

"Remember we originally bought the island from Detroit for $1 billion, about $1 million an acre. That money was raised by a consortium of Wall Street banks and private equity groups. In addition to the land purchase, money was raised for the various costs of planning and the interest carry on the original investment. The investors were promised a preferred return and expected to be paid back over a 30-year period. The investors were also given first opportunities to buy land for their office centers they intended to build on Belle Isle. That was part of the deal. But the clincher and what really excited the Wall Street crowd was the promise that their managers and investment bankers would be guaranteed citizenship."

"Why was that important to them?"

"Well, remember they were mostly New York or New Jersey residents, some from Connecticut. These were all high tax states and we had already established in our constitution, there would be no income taxes. Not all wanted to move, but many did. So we had our first 'customers' lined up, before we evened opened our doors.

"But back to the property tax question. It was easy to start to value the land, as Belle Isle was basically vacant, so whatever was paid for it was totally attributed to the actions of government. We had established our constitution, form of government, tax system and so forth. We also had master planned the island into the various zones of office, commercial/retail, schools, and residential. We set prices on each area according to its use and location. The river views commanded higher prices. Where we allowed taller buildings, the prices were higher. You get the idea.

"Then as the land sales proceeded, we adjusted our prices to meet the market. Some of our tracts sold faster than expected, so we increased the prices on those areas. On those that sold slowly, we lowered the prices. So we had real pricing information on which to base our land values for property tax purposes. And when we increased or lowered prices based on a sale, then all the similar properties' land values were adjusted accordingly. Basically the same comparable sales system used on the old system, but we applied it on a land value-only basis."

"But Darin, once all the land is taken and you don't have any vacant land sales, then what do you use for land value?"

"Joe, when a sale takes place, we basically subtract the value of the building and improvements from the sale price and take the remainder as the land value. The assessor uses tables to calculate the depreciated value of the building.

"For example, let's say you bought a lot for R$200,000 and built a house on it for R$800,000. Your total cost including the land is R$1,000,000. You pay taxes only on the R$200,000 initially. Seven years later, you sell the house and lot to a new buyer for R$1,200,000. The house is seven years old now and let's say you haven't put any improvements into the house, only maintained it. We assume the house has depreciated in value, from our studies of house values over the last 100 years. The average decrease in real value is about 1.4% per year for the reason that buyer preferences change — floor plans change, kitchens become larger or more recently smaller as people aren't cooking as much, closets and bathrooms change in size and configuration, skylights come and go, technology changes, all kinds of things change. So we apply that depreciation schedule to your house and say your house is now worth about 10 percent less than what it cost to build. So now your house by itself is worth the original cost of R$800,000 less 10 percent or about R$720,000. So the land is the balance. R$1,200,000 less R$720,000 equals R$480,000. So land value has increased from R$200,000 to R$480,000 over the seven-year period. So the new buyer would pay taxes on $480,000, but also all owners of similar sized lots would see their assessed land values be adjusted accordingly. But keep in mind this transaction would be one of many, and all the transactions would be considered and averaged out.

"Also, that doesn't mean the buyer's taxes would go up that much, if at all. Because the taxes are based on how much we spend on government, not how much we *could* take in. In fact, the taxes may go down, depending on what is happening on other types of real estate. We automatically adjust the rate each year based on the total assessed value and the annual spending budget. And remember, if government isn't doing a good job, there would be *no* increase in land value. When a property owner sees a real increase in value, they are happy, believe me."

"How about if the homeowner makes improvements during that seven year period — let's say an addition?"

"Then we increase the building value by our estimate of what was spent on the improvements and apply the depreciation schedule separately to that improvement. That way, there is no increase in land value due to what was spent on the improvements. We have similar schedules for remodeling.

"On commercial properties, we use the same approach. Businesses depreciate in real value also; buyer preferences change and buildings become obsolete. In the case of this class of commercial buildings, the figure is about two percent per year. So let's say in the case of Andrew's restaurant, he sells it after a 10-year hold for what he paid for it. The building value is now 20 percent less and the land has increased by the same dollar amount. What caused the land to increase in value? For a restaurateur, it increased because government did a great job in attracting new residents who are his customers, for providing clean, safe and heated streets, and good transportation to move customers to his restaurant. We are not making adjustments without information. When a business changes hands, then we have a 'comp', which we apply, in conjunction with other sales, to all similar properties."

Joe's head was swimming with figures.

"I'm a doctor, not a mathematician. But it seems to me Andrew can argue that his great food and service caused the value to go up, not something government did."

"I'm sure Andrew would argue that and if you remember my brother, he's not shy about engaging in argument. But remember, we are valuing classes of property *equally*, with a number of data points, not just off one transaction. So Andrew's hypothetical sale would be just one data point in all the sales in the restaurant/entertainment district. Also, if his restaurant increases in sales and profits over time, at least *some* of the effect is due to the fact people want to come to the district to eat and shop and so forth. Our part in that is to provide a safe, pleasing street environment. The basic principle here is you pay us for what we do for you and don't pay us for what you do for yourself."

They continued chatting over dinner, reminiscing about high school at Detroit Country Day. Joe played football for Country Day while Darin had skied and both kept in touch with a number of their old teammates.

A solidly built man approached their table with a wide smile. Joe immediately recognized Darin's brother Andrew. Andrew was four years older than Darin, but like

Darin, looked younger than his age. Joe rose to his feet and they exchanged a hug.

"Joe, or should I call you Dr. Sharif?" Andrew grinned. "Welcome to my humble maison. It's good to see you."

"Humble, hardly!" Joe retorted with a big smile. "It's beautiful, but I appreciate the attempt at modesty."

"Actually, I can't take much credit. Darin's Belle Isle Planning Department had a heavy hand on the exterior design — man what a pain in the butt they were!

Darin answered, "Oh get over it. You know you love the way it looks."

Andrew joined them at their table and they continued talking about the old days at Country Day. After dinner, Andrew ordered a 20-year-old Port and shared a glass with Darin. Joe had a coffee.

"Well, I'm going to get back to work." Andrew got up to leave. "And dinner is on the house tonight. It's so good to see you."

They embraced one more time and Andrew disappeared.

Back on the monorail, Joe marveled at the views as they sped around the island. The sun had just set and the buildings were bathed in the warm glow of the street lights. As the monorail turned to the west, the Detroit

Yacht Club passed below to their right. Past the Yacht Club was the beach. Some young couples were sitting on the sand around a fire pit ablaze with burning logs. Up ahead, Joe could see the twin towers of the Four Seasons, with its blue lights running up its sides. He wished he had his camera but knew a picture would never match the memory. In a few minutes they were back at the Four Seasons. They decided to meet at 10 the next morning and Joe exited through the monorail's doors.

## CHAPTER 7

*Liberty, when it begins to take root, is a plant of rapid growth.*

*-George Washington*

## DAY TWO

Joe was a few minutes late as he entered the coffee shop off the lobby of the Four Seasons. Darin was seated at a table in the corner busy on his PDA, apparently on a video-conference call, wearing ear-buds and a low volume mike. He looked up, motioned Joe to have a seat and quickly finished his call.

"Good morning. How'd you sleep?"

"Great. I feel like a new man. And the communication center in the room worked great — even a doctor could figure it out!"

"Yeah, yeah — so Damascus is still standing?"

"Yes sir, sometimes I feel like they would rather not have me around. I get in the way."

"I know the feeling, but it's a good one. It means you've trained your staff well."

"I hope so. By the way, what is behind the name 'Von Mises Suite'?"

Darin answered, "Oh — Von Mises. He was an economist from the Austrian school of economics. His full name is Ludwig Von Mises. He was born in the early 1800's in Austria-Hungary, what is now the Ukraine. He was fluent in four languages plus Latin, studied at the University of Vienna and got a doctorate in economics. Being Jewish, he fled Europe at the start of World War II and settled in New York City. He taught at N.Y.U. well into his 80's and died in 1973 at age 92. Mises wrote that socialism must fail because it had no pricing system and prices are absolutely needed to allocate resources to what people want. That's the short version of a complex economic theory. Mises influenced many people including Ayn Rand, the novelist who wrote 'Atlas Shrugged' and 'Fountainhead' — we named our currency after her."

Darin continued, "We always try to name important things after people who espoused our core principles. So we have rooms named after free market economists, currency after a free market novelist and some buildings after famous architects and some of our streets after leaders of our founding group. But one thing you will never see is anything named after an elected official. What kind of craziness would that be?"

The waitress brought Turkish coffee and an assortment of Danish and fruit.

"So Darin, what's on the agenda today? I hope I'm not getting in the way of your work."

"Not at all.  I have the day-to-day done by others.  My time is blocked off for you.  This morning, we are touring the Service Center and after lunch, we're going over to the business district to tour one of the investment firms. If we have time, we'll stop by Andrew's office.  I've got some nap time for you later in the afternoon and then we're having dinner at my place.  I've invited a few friends to join us.  They want to meet you."


The weather was warm with a light breeze so they walked to the Service Center, which was less than a mile to the east.  They walked in the middle of the street as did others — although Joe noted there were sidewalks on both sides.  Joe hadn't seen a car, only people on foot, some bicycles and an occasional mini-vehicle, which resembled a golf cart, with four seats and a sunroof.

## CHAPTER 8

*The truth has no agenda.*

*-Unknown*


## STREET DESIGN


"Darin, are cars not allowed on Belle Isle? It's so quiet compared to Damascus!"


"Actually cars are allowed on Belle Isle, but only once a year and they have to be Formula One race cars," Darin answered with a smile.


"Many of our residents have cars, but they keep them at the Transportation Center and use the monorail to access them."


"Then why do you have a street, rather than a wide pedestrian sidewalk?"


"Two reasons. As I mentioned, we spent a lot of time on the master planning for Belle Isle. We studied other micro countries for ideas and one we looked at closely was Monaco. Monaco is one half the size of Belle Isle — they have less than 22 million square feet of land area and we have almost 43 million. Their population is 33,000 people and ours is designed up to 50,000, so our population density is less than theirs. We have some opportunities for a little more open space and we use it, as you will see. But one of our early objectives was to put Belle Isle on the world map, particularly as we wanted to attract international investment firms to put their North American headquarters here. So cultural issues matter to us and we thought that having a world-class racing event here would appeal to the younger crowd who are the movers and shakers in the money world.

"So our primary street is basically designed as a race course, with some straightaways, turns, an esse, a chicane, and the whole bit. We hired a couple of prominent Formula One drivers to consult on the design. It's worked out well and race week here is one of the highlights of the summer season.

"We also have secondary streets but they are narrower, just wide enough for service vehicles to deliver fresh produce, pick up the trash, deliver building materials and construction equipment, for fire trucks, ambulances and so forth. But the non-emergency vehicles are only allowed to travel on the streets from 3 a.m. to 7 a.m. And we have severe noise restrictions, so they are very quiet. Of course emergency vehicles are allowed at any time and they have sirens to warn people off the streets.

"The other vehicles allowed deal with snow removal, but they aren't needed generally in the high pedestrian traffic areas such as the shopping/entertainment district, because the streets and sidewalks are heated in those areas."

"Isn't that expensive?"

"Yes and no. We started with natural gas, which heated an anti-freeze liquid flowing through pipes buried beneath the streets. But more recently, a company on the Detroit side of the river built a small plant that turns clean coal into a coal-gas product. That reduced our costs about 40%. We still have the natural gas as a back-up."

"Darin, in Damascus, we have a lot of concrete walks, streets and buildings. I haven't seen any concrete here. What gives?"

"Concrete doesn't meet our aesthetic test. So we don't allow any use of it. If it is used for structural reasons, it has to have an exterior material added to hide it, or if in small amounts we allow it to be tinted. You notice the street is made of asphalt, which is actually to Formula One specs. The sidewalks are comprised of many different materials that complement and integrate with the facades of the buildings they serve. When a property owner submits architectural plans for his building, he also submits his sidewalk materials he proposes to use. So you notice as we are walking here, the sidewalks are changing. Some brick pavers, some slate, different stones. We only require that they look good, meet smoothness standards and of course are wide enough. It's an approach Carmel, California uses."

"It looks great!"

"Thanks, one could say our concrete prohibition is a sort of a political statement. In the Soviet era, the Russians built the ugliest buildings in the world using primarily concrete. So we figure concrete and communism are linked. Not here! In our free market world, we go the other direction. We value beauty. I also might add we can afford it. The Soviets couldn't."

## CHAPTER 9

*Progress starts with the truth.*

*-Dan Sullivan*


## CITIZENSHIP


They were interrupted by a siren. Joe looked up and saw an ambulance coming down the street, heading toward the bridge to the mainland. Pedestrians were clearing the street to make a path and stopped and watched. Most of them were clapping and a few were cheering. Attached to the top of the ambulance was a pink balloon. Joe looked at Darin, "What's happening?"


Darin replied, "A woman is having a baby and they're probably heading to the Detroit Medical Center or perhaps Henry Ford Hospital. Many of our deliveries take place off the island. If the ambulance operator knows ahead of time what the sex of the baby is, they tie a balloon with the appropriate color. If not, they do a blue and a pink. The people on the street are clapping because they know soon we are going to have another Belle Islander among us."


Joe asked, "You say another Belle Islander, but this baby will be born in the U.S. and therefore will be a U.S. citizen, right?"


"No, we have in our arrangements with the U.S. that Belle Isle citizenship is based on having a citizen parent. If a person is born on the island, that does not automatically entitle them to be a Belle Isle citizen. They have to have a parent who is. It's modeled after the Swiss system. Of course, we also have a naturalization process. All our original citizens were 'naturalized' as are the current immigrants."

"How does someone become a citizen, if not born into it?"

"They apply to our Citizenship Board. The Citizenship Board is comprised of three members who review applications. During busy times we have more than one Board going. The majority of our applications come from the U.S., but we have many also from France and Great Britain, some from Canada and quite a few from Central and South America, even Asia."

"What are the requirements?"

"Well, first of all they can't be a criminal escaping from somewhere. Also, they have to have paid their bills and have good credit. That applies to everyone. Then most prospects have to make a substantial contribution of capital either directly to the Belle Isle Treasury or to a business based on Belle Isle."

"What kind of contribution are we talking about?"

"For a direct contribution, it's several hundred thousand Rand, I don't recall the exact number today. For a business, it's higher."

"That seems like a lot."

"It is, but remember, we paid a big sum to buy the island from Detroit, then had to put in the infrastructure — the roads, the monorail, utilities and so forth. We did this by raising money with bonds that are repaid from the citizenship fees. We also have purchased commodities that back up the Rand with those fees. And keep in mind, we have more applications then we have openings."

"But it seems to me you end up with only rich people. It sounds pretty exclusionary."

"We hold 20 percent of our citizenship spots open for 'exceptions.' These are people who cannot afford the standard contribution, but have some other attribute that we think will benefit Belle Isle. So we have 'starving artists,' some talented musicians, some teachers with special knowledge. For example, we had an application a few years back from an Italian gentleman who was a master stonecutter in Italy. He had read about some of our architectural goals here and wrote to say he wanted to help. He now is teaching his craft to others on the island at one of our trade schools. As you walk around the island, you'll see some of his work, it's just amazing. He didn't have the standard contribution, but came anyway."

Darin continued, "And we have some people who came here with absolutely nothing. Nothing but a burning desire to take advantage of the unlimited opportunity that Belle Isle offers. People who ask for nothing but a chance to make a better life for themselves and their family. You'll meet one of them at my home tonight over dinner. Hector Cabrera. Hector was from Mexico. Came here dirt poor. Great story.

"Another group of people who apply are the entrepreneurs. Many are from other continents who have a business that is either being hugely over taxed or is in danger of being nationalized. They know there are no business taxes and absolutely no risk of the government getting into their shorts here. Did I tell you, Belle Isle is ranked number one in the world in terms of business climate and political risk? These entrepreneurs come here with a plan and expertise, often little else. They meet with the financial types who are based here, raise their capital and start or continue their business. Often they take office space for their administrative and engineering functions, but then look for industrial land to build a factory. We have very little industrial land on the island, because we don't have the room, so the factories are getting built across the river in Detroit. They want their manufacturing plants to be close where they can be supervised, not in China or somewhere far away. In fact, many of these folks *are* from China. They left China because the government was in their face. One of our biggest success stories is a Chinese family that makes retinal activated screens for PDAs – they engineer on Belle Isle, build in Detroit and ship all over the world.

"So quite a bit of the abandoned land in old Detroit is now becoming industrial park with brand new buildings and so forth. These new plants employ a lot of people from Detroit. And Detroit and Southeast Michigan have come roaring back with all the investment."

# CHAPTER 10

*Government is not reason; it is not eloquent; it is force.*
*Like fire, it is a dangerous servant and a fearful master.*

*-George Washington*

## SERVICE CENTER  I

The Service Center loomed on their left.  It was a three-story building largely made of stucco and stone.  Brick pavers welcomed visitors to the large doors.  Above the portico were the words, "Belle Isle Service Center."

Darin noticed Joe's gaze at the entry.

"We don't call it the Government building.  We use the term 'Service Center.'  Words mean things and we try to use simple words and phrases to set the tone of our mission, which is to serve our citizens; to work for them.  We try to reinforce that at every opportunity.  One of the trends in the U.S. was the advent of the 'Ruling Class.'  People resented it and government's approval rating was abysmal.  We try to go the other direction, having a bottom up government rather than a top down."

He continued as they entered the building.  "Here we have police, fire, administration, courts and the jail.  Administration includes assessment and taxes, records, planning and building, and charitable support.  I have my office here."

They took the elevator up to the third floor and entered through a door marked "Administration" and continued down a hallway to an area designated as "Planning and Building." Past a reception desk was an open area with work cubicles, separated by moveable partitions. Joe counted four people in front of computer screens. To the left was a large conference room with various plans and renderings adorning the walls. On the right were some doors leading to offices. Darin led Joe into one of them. To the right of the door was a small sign that simply said, "Darin Fraser." There was no job title or position described.

Joe was surprised how small Darin's office was. For someone as famous as Darin had become and the guiding force behind such a successful country, Joe expected a more grandiose office. It couldn't have been more than 10' x 12' and had a single desk with a monitor and two guest chairs. A window looked out to the south, but the view of the river was blocked by the backs of various high-rise buildings. A Schefflera plant was in the corner near the window, soaking up the morning sun. Darin grabbed two waters from a small refrigerator, handed one to Joe and sat down behind his desk and motioned Joe to sit in the facing guest chair.

Darin recognized the look of bewilderment on Joe's face. He'd seen it many times before.

"Yeah, I know it's small. Remember, I'm a servant of the people. I work for them. I'm spending their money. So they have the best views from their homes or apartments, the nicest offices if they choose to pay for them. I actually have everything I need here to do my job. Notice the video camera feeds. I can hook up here with the best consultants in the world with a few key strokes on the computer and talk to them in person. It works very well. It's all I need."

# CHAPTER 11

*There are two educations.  One should teach us how to make a living and the other how to live.*

*-John Adams*

## CULTURE AND RECREATION

There was a large monitor on the wall opposite the window.  Darin punched a few keys on his computer and a slide show started.  It ran about eight minutes and talked about the recent history of Belle Isle, the mission of the community and the philosophies and approaches used in the planning and design.  Being ranked number one in the world for business climate and political risk was mentioned more than once.  Darin's voice moderated the show and at the end, he appeared on the roof of the Four Seasons, giving his closing remarks.  It was well done.

"We use this as our puff piece when drumming up interest for businesses that are considering locating here.  Of course, quality of life is very important, so that's why we emphasize our schools and recreation, the boating and the cultural events, both here and in Detroit.  We talk about the history of Belle Isle and how we have refurbished the Belle Isle Aquarium, which is the oldest aquarium in the United States.  We value history and have saved and fixed up many of the historical structures.

"We also have some great tourist and entertainment events going on all year.  I already mentioned the Formula One race.  The race is in June and all the restaurants and hotels are absolutely packed.  Many of the restaurants along the race course have outdoor sun decks that make for popular viewing spots. The international reporters give us a lot of press all over the world. It's good for business.

"In July, we have the Thunderbolt hydroplane races, which are a Detroit River tradition and very popular.

"In August, we have the Red Bull air races where the aerobatic racers fly around pylons just to our west.

"In September, we have our Independence Day 5K/10K races. We still celebrate the U.S.'s July 4th with fireworks and the like, but we also celebrate our own Independence Day, which is September 14th. So we have a race that day and it attracts all kinds of runners, both Belle Islanders and Detroiters. Some runners and their friends even come in from Chicago. In early October, we have the Detroit Free Press Marathon, which runs through Detroit, Windsor and Belle Isle.

"Also in October, we have Halloween of course and have a lot of fun doing it. It's become a tradition for shopkeepers and restaurant staff to dress up in costumes. They do their normal business but also encourage young trick-or-treaters to come in and grab special treats on their walk around the island.

"In December, on the evening of the 23rd informal groups of carolers tour the downtown and sing Christmas carols outside the shops and restaurants. It's a big festival night and most restaurants are serving on the outside sun decks that night. People are dressed in their winter clothes, eating whatever and drinking Schnapps while being serenaded. I'm not sure who has more fun that evening, the carolers or the carolees!

"But the most fun event of the year is the Winterfest. We don't have the international crowd the Formula One Race attracts, but it's a very lively group. We hold it at the end of January, when the weather is the coldest. It's a three-day gig starting on a Friday afternoon and ending on Sunday. Friday evening we have an outdoor hockey game featuring two of the top college hockey teams in the U.S. We play it at the football field in the Sports Complex. We only have seating for 10,000 people, so tickets are hard to get and we are sold out years ahead.

"In Parc de Leon, our park near downtown, we have the ice sculpture festival. One of our sponsors is Credit Suisse. They donate R$25,000 in prize money so some of the best ice sculptors from around the world come in for it. It is absolutely amazing what they can do. Last year someone carved Belle Isle itself, with a lot of architectural detail!

"But the highlight of the Winterfest, in my opinion, is the Sled Dog Marathon. This starts on Saturday at 9 p.m. and runs all night along the Formula One course right through downtown and around the island. In preparation for it, we shut down the street heating system a week ahead and truck in and spread snow on the course if we need to. The dogs run all night and finish up 12 hours later. Whoever has run the farthest is the winner. Again, there is significant donor support and prize money, so teams come from Alaska and the Yukon. We set up temporary dog shelters in one of the parks for the dogs. This event is so popular, the restaurants and bars stay open all night as the fans cheer on their favorites.

The drivers and dogs come in to town about a week early, so by race time, many of the Islanders have come to know them personally and they cheer loudly for their favorites, and a lot of wagering takes place!"

## CHAPTER 12

*Status quo, you know, is Latin for "the mess we're in."*
*-Ronald Reagan*


## DETROIT


Darin continued, "Also, as you notice, we talk about Detroit and what it has to offer in the way of theatre, arts, restaurants, entertainment and of course, sports. Detroit is a very important part of our promotion of the island. And it's quite accessible. You can get door-to-door to downtown in about 20 minutes from Belle Isle."


"So how is Detroit doing? When I left, it was really in a bad way."


"It's gone through a lot of change. From 2010-2020, Detroit lost a tremendous amount of population, going from about 750,000 people down to less than 500,000.


"How did Detroit turn itself around?" Joe asked.


"It wasn't easy. There were so many problems. High crime, high spending, poor city services, all made worse by extremely low population density. In 2010, Detroit had 5,000 people per square mile; Chicago had 12,000.


"The public unions fought any attempts at real reform. There were agreements made between the city and the state to make changes, but these agreements were soon violated. Nothing seemed to work. Finally the inevitable happened."

"What was that?"

"Detroit was put into bankruptcy. But it was quite different than other municipal bankruptcies. Call it a 'destructuring bankruptcy.' The state put together a plan to unincorporate Detroit and replace it with a collection of smaller cities. Each of the smaller cities was chosen based on its neighborhood identity and the fact it had property values that could support services. So now we have the communities of Palmer Woods, East Village, Jefferson, Corktown, Wayne State, Mexican Village, among others. The City of Detroit remains but is now the downtown area with the sports stadiums, theaters, restaurants, office and some residential. Detroit proper has about 45,000 people within its new city limits, but the overall area is still known as Greater Detroit.

"These new cities have their own city governments, police forces and taxation rates. They are now much more accountable than under the old system. And they have a population density which can support these services efficiently.

"Those areas of old Detroit which did not become part of the new cities were turned into farms, forest and parks. They're called 'green zones.' The billion dollars which was received from the sale of Belle Isle helped fund the relocation of residents from green zones to the new cities.

"The plan was put together with the help of urban planning experts, endorsed by the state and presented to the bankruptcy judge. It was quickly approved. Then the positive changes started to happen and they happened rather quickly."

Joe asked, "Tell me more about the new Detroit. You say people have moved back?"

"Yes. They are mostly younger professionals who live in lofts and rehabbed buildings. They come from all races, attracted by the culture, so Detroit is now an integrated city. I've talked a lot to these so-called urban pioneers and have gotten a good feel for what has attracted them to Detroit. They speak of the great old buildings in the city. Detroit has some of the coolest architecture that is found only in cities like New York or Chicago. Detroit borders Canada, which gives it an international flavor. The Detroit River and the surrounding connected lakes make Detroit both a major shipping and commerce link plus offers lots of recreation opportunities. And the city has an artistic Bohemian culture, which combined with its music makes it a cool place to be. Some attribute the spark that revitalized Detroit to the cool bars of that era like the Café D'Mongo Speakeasy. Young people loved those places. And when they married and had kids, many stayed because there were, and are now, many good private and public schools. The old Detroit Public School system is gone. What turned the corner for these communities was having their own taxation and police departments. The crime, bad schools, high taxes and corruption of the old Detroit killed it. The new cities that replaced old Detroit are much more efficient and accountable. Once that happened, people started moving back."

"This is all good then, right?"

"Absolutely. We need Detroit. Detroit's the cultural anchor for the area, including Belle Isle. It's one of the few cities on the continent that has a major league team in every sport — baseball, football, basketball and hockey. Plus a world class art museum, opera house, symphony and theaters.

"But Detroit needs Belle Isle, too. First of all, our citizens comprise a major donor base to these institutions. But more importantly, Belle Isle's reputation, which is now world-wide, has attracted tremendous investment to the area. High tech manufacturing has added thousands of jobs on the Detroit side of the river. There are businesses headquartered on Belle Isle, but they manufacture in Detroit. Have you heard of the Siccatta watch?"

"I think so. Is that the watch that listens, talks, can read your eyes and do all sorts of things? Sort of a watch/PDA combination? I think they are selling some in Syria now."

"Yes, that's it. Well, they are all made here in Detroit. Detroit may become the new Switzerland!

"Also, Detroiters have largely built Belle Isle. We've created thousands upon thousands of new jobs, particularly for the construction industry as we built the new hotels, restaurants, schools, churches, homes, the monorail — you name it. Everything from scratch. During the construction heyday, our national tree was the construction crane! And now we have all kinds of permanent jobs, many of which are filled by Detroiters."


Darin continued, "And back on the Detroit side of the river, the farming that is done in the green zones is very interesting. As society has moved to healthier organic foods, the trend has been to grow healthy strains of various fruits, vegetables and even meat products. This doesn't lend itself to the mass-farming methods used in Iowa and other farming states that have large tracts of land. It requires more hand work and personal attention.


"I think I mentioned to you my brother Andrew grows specialty tomatoes. Well, that is done largely by hand on one of the Detroit farms. He employs a lot of people. Many are former prisoners who are re-entering society and developing work skills. The tomatoes are shipped each morning during the harvest season to our market, along with other farmers' products. We have our own farmers' market on the island and most of the stuff is grown on the Detroit farms. Andrew also uses those tomatoes in his salsa products.


"So between the construction jobs, the new factories and specialty farming, Detroit is coming back big time. On the Detroit side of the bridge, a whole new community has sprung up, called Jefferson. It has all kinds of shopping, businesses and residential. We were all surprised how fast it happened. But I tell you, it's all about attitude. You let people see, feel and taste unlimited opportunity — well, just step aside and get out of the way. Otherwise you get run over."

## CHAPTER 13

*Be thankful we're not getting all the government we're paying for.*

*-Will Rogers*

## SERVICE CENTER II

Darin and Joe finished their waters and left Darin's office to continue the tour. Passing by an office marked "Accounting," Darin stuck his head in and motioned Joe to follow. Sitting at his desk was an older man of African descent staring intently at his computer screen. Darin introduced Herbert Watson to Joe.

"Herbert heads our accounting department here. He makes sure everyone gets paid on time and keeps the Island's books straight. Meet Dr. Joe Sharif. He came all the way from Syria to see us."

Herbert rose and greeted Joe with a broad smile. "We're truly honored by your visit. Darin has been talking about it for weeks. I finally get to place a face with the name."

"Well thank you. You all have been very kind."

Darin spoke, "Herbert, I'm having Joe over for dinner at my place tonight and would like you to join us if you're free. Tom Williams is coming and maybe John Miller. Can you make it?"

"Can't man. My wife has tickets tonight at the Fox. Otherwise would have loved to."

"Understood. It *is* short notice. Next time."

Directly next to Herbert's office was Assessments and Taxes. Upon entering the reception area, Joe was struck by the collage of pictures on the walls depicting the various activities that were done with the taxes collected. Many were Norman Rockwell paintings, such as the policeman sitting next to the runaway kid at the soda bar. Others were actual photos. One was an ambulance transporting a patient to the Medical Center. Another was a fireman with a soot blackened face shooting a stream of water from a hose on a burning house.

Darin smiled, "Here is where people come to appeal their assessments, so we figured why not do a little marketing on where their money goes to put them in a better mood.

"Also, since transparency is important to us, we post the pay schedule and job descriptions of all Service Center employees right here on this board. So the taxpayers again know where their money is going. We also post the budget for all Service Center activities."

"Don't the employees feel their privacy is a bit violated, with everyone knowing what they make?"

"At first. But now they accept it. We stress that transparency is essential in the public areas to earn the public trust. If they want to keep their pay private, they need to work in the private sector."

Walking past reception, they came to an open area with a woman working on a computer.

"Sheila is keeping the tax assessments current, based on transaction data. She sends out all the new assessments each year by February 1$^{st}$. Over here, we have the conference and appeals room. We have appeals in the first two weeks of February. The Board of Appeals is comprised of three citizens who are appointed for overlapping three year terms by the president and confirmed by the Council. The Board of Appeals members are paid a nominal amount for their time."

"Do you get many appeals?"

"Oh, about 10 on average, sometimes a few more. As we base the raw land value on an algorithm backed by actual data, it's pretty cut and dry. As I mentioned before, everyone is taxed the same based on computed land values. It's pretty hard to argue with it. But of course, we take everyone's appeal seriously and sometimes we make mistakes."

# CHAPTER 14

*Socialism, like the ancient ideas from which it springs,
confuses the distinction between government and society.
As a result of this, every time we object to a thing being
done by government, the socialists conclude that we object
to its being done at all.*

*-Frederic Bastiat*

## CHARITABLE SUPPORT

The last door on the third floor hallway was marked
"Charitable Support." Like the others, it had a small reception area with walls sprinkled with photos of people
helping other people. One was a man dressed like Santa
Claus with a large bag slung over his shoulder surrounded by a small group of children. Another showed a
young smiling girl holding a puppy and next to it was a
framed photo of a Salvation Army kettle with some Salvation soldiers. It was signed by a Salvation Army Colo-
nel.

"This department's mission is to support charitable
work. We have virtually no government involvement in
the traditional social safety net. But most of us believe
that everyone should have adequate food, shelter, education and health care. We just leave it to the charitable
sector to supply these things for the less fortunate.
What we do is promote and foster support for the charities that provide those things. Charities that engage in
fund raising here have to register with us and provide
documentation for our approval if they want to have our
certification and support. "

"What kind of documentation do they have to provide?"

"Well, their purpose and mission, of course. Then, also their annual operating budget and audited financial statements that show all the salaries of paid staff, the number of paid staff hours and volunteer hours, what percentage of their revenue is spent on fund raising and the like. Also, and this is very important, what key metrics have they established to measure their effectiveness? For example, for a food program, how many meals did they serve? For health care support, how many patients were seen? And the metrics have to be audited also. What we are trying to do is to make sure money is being raised efficiently and that the money is well spent on the intended purpose, and not soaked up by excessive overhead and salaries. We actually issue ratings based on our analysis, sort of like Moody's or Standard & Poor's would do for a corporation. But because we are a small country with limited staff, we monitor and issue ratings for only about 20 charities."

"But Darin, I guess I don't understand. In the U.S., charities are designated as such, which allows contributions to them to be tax deductible. But since one doesn't pay any income tax here, why does it matter? I assume people are free to give money to whomever they want. So what is the advantage of a charity to have a good rating?"

"Two reasons. First, people here are busy and many don't have the time to carefully research the effectiveness of a charity. So they rely on us to help them in making their determination. Second, we actually allocate part of our tax revenue to direct financial support of the charities if the donations fall short. But we don't determine which organizations get the money. Our citizens do that through an online vote. There is a website that lists all the charities including their ratings and details. Four times a year, our citizens on a particular voting day go to the website, review the data and ratings and make a percentage allocation of their vote for their favorite charities. Think of it like the old 401(k) investments our fathers had, where they allocated 20% of their investment to this stock and 15% to that stock or bond and so forth. Well, we follow the same process here. And of course people only have one vote. And some don't vote at all."

"It sounds a little complicated."

"Not really. It's quite simple and works well."

"How much of the general budget goes to charitable support?"

"About 10 percent. And we're considering cutting it back because we have accumulated quite a surplus."

They headed to the elevator and got off on the second floor.

# CHAPTER 15

*Pure democracy is two foxes and a chicken deciding what to have for dinner.*

*-Unknown*

## SERVICE CENTER III

"This is the floor where we have the courts and the jail. There are three courtrooms and housing for about 25 prisoners."

Darin opened one of the courtroom doors and quietly walked in, motioning Joe to join him. They took a seat on one of the back benches. The courtroom resembled those Joe had seen in the U.S., with a judge behind the bench up on a raised platform and a witness chair near-by. In front were two tables with some lawyers and a jury box set to the right. In the jury box were two men and a woman, all who looked to be in their 60's or 70's.

The lawyers were arguing what appeared to be a medical malpractice case. Joe watched with interest. Even though it was an obstetrical case, he knew all the terms and quickly caught the gist of the case. Apparently, the plaintiff was a woman who had delivered a child who later developed epilepsy. The obstetrician was being sued as a result. The plaintiff's lawyer had just wrapped up his opening statement and the defense attorney was now showing the medical records to the court. The jurors watched with interest, passing the logs among them as the attorney went through his arguments.

Darin whispered, "The courts have different rules here. I'll explain when we get outside."

They watched for another half hour until the Court recessed for lunch.

"Let's finish the tour on the first floor, then we'll get some lunch on our own."

On the first floor were police and fire, anti-corruption, the president's office and the council chamber.

"Joe, I'll show you the Council Chamber. The police, fire and president's offices are rather ordinary. I think the police force numbers 25 policemen and administrative support staff, we have eight trained firefighters but only two are on duty at a time, the others have day jobs and are on call. The president has a vice president, who is really like an executive assistant and one other staff member. Anti-corruption has a staff of two and they have fairly high security. They don't give public tours."

Darin and Joe walked through some large doors into a small assembly room. On the back wall was a flag and a large plaque with an inscription in Latin, which Joe couldn't read. There was a large wide seated podium area with ten seats and the names of the officials in front. A speaker's podium faced the legislators' platform. Behind the speaker's podium was audience seating for perhaps 80 people.

The Council members meet once a month on a Tuesday night from about 7 p.m. to 10 p.m. or so. The meetings are recorded and telecast. You can pick it up on your TV on the community channel. It's organized much like a typical city hall in the U.S."

"Are the meetings well attended?"

"Not really. Ten people would be a big turnout. We get more at budget time. Actually many times, there is nothing on the agenda and the meeting is cancelled. But sometimes we get some controversial land use issues and the turnout is greater."

Off the first floor lobby was a cafeteria. Darin and Joe grabbed some sandwiches and took them out the back to an outside dining area where they were shaded from the sun by a pergola made from lattice intertwined with vines. Other service center workers were relaxing in the noon day sun, quietly talking among themselves. Joe was starting to feel a lull, the fatigue from his long trip and different time zone weighing on him.

Darin noticed. "Hey old man, you look like you're a prospect for an afternoon siesta. We'll give you a nap break after lunch. The tour can take a break."

"I'm hanging in there. Let's keep going. This is too interesting."

"Great. I'm glad you think so, but if you need a rest let me know."

"Darin, are you still a vegetarian?"  Darin was munching on a veggie sandwich.

"Yup.  Since high school, but not a vegan, that's over the top for me."

"Well, I try to eat healthy too.  Being in the medical field, I see all the bad things bad food can do to you.  Say, speaking of medicine, what was going on in the court-room?  You said the rules were different."

## CHAPTER 16

*He who knows best knows how little he knows.*

*-Thomas Jefferson*

## COURT PROCEDURES

"Yes, well we were seeing a civil case. The same court-room and judges hear criminal cases too. On the criminal side, the rules are pretty much the same as the U.S., with regard to defendants' rights, rules of evidence and so forth. But our criminal laws are somewhat simpler.

"On the civil side though, our rules are quite different. In technical matters, we figure the common man doesn't have the training and expertise to understand and make good judgments in today's increasingly complex world. That's not a form of elitism; it's just recognizing that our world has become increasingly specialized.

"So for instance, in the trial we observed, the jury was made up of three physicians who are expert in the matter being tried. In fact, they were probably all OB-GYN's. Usually they are retired and have the time and interest to serve as jurors. Both sides have the opportunity to interview and challenge prospective jurors, so the three who actually served have been vetted by both sides. If one of the lawyers ends up rejecting all the candidates, the judge has the authority to step in and appoint them.

"Another difference with a typical U.S. system is how lawyers get the cases. In the U.S., on personal injury cases a lawyer approaches a prospective plaintiff or gets approached and tries to sign them up with a 1/3 contingency fee. Often the lawyers advertise to solicit cases. We think that the lawyers often get rich in the process, leaving the plaintiffs with less money than they could otherwise get or deserve and the 1/3 contingency fee amounts to price fixing. So what we do is encourage aggrieved parties to put their case out to bid. One of our rated and supported charities provides an initial screening service for cases. A person calls a phone number, gives the details of the case in a telephone interview and that information is posted on a website for prospective plaintiff's attorneys to bid on. They could bid a fixed fee, a 1/3 contingency or any other percentage they feel is appropriate. On some potential big cases, the attorneys bid 10 percent or lower. Along with the bid, the attorneys submit their resumes and their prior trial history with regard to similar cases and the outcomes. Then that information is transmitted back to the potential plaintiff, who makes a decision to go forward with a particular attorney or perhaps to interview several of them."

"That certainly sounds like a more open and free market approach to litigation."

"There's more. One of the items our courts do *not* allow to be discovered is the amount of medical malpractice insurance the physician carries. We figure the ability to pay shouldn't play into it. The case needs to be decided on its merits. Now, if the physician chooses to disclose with the approval of the insurance company, then the insurance may be disclosed. Sometimes that's done, sometimes not. It varies."

Joe queried, "Is there more?"

"Yes, the loser pays the court costs and the other attorney's charges within reason of course. It keeps down the questionable cases."

"So how has this affected the insurance premiums the doctors pay?"

"It has reduced them greatly. Most doctors pay only one-fifth of what the premiums would be in the U.S., unless they have a high claim history and the insurance companies give them poor ratings."

"Darin, that sounds great. I know my father always complained about his premiums in the U.S., and he wasn't in a high risk specialty."

"Yes, and the lower premiums have translated to lower pricing, as the doctors costs are lower. And we use the same system on other technical specialties, where the average person isn't conversant enough with the issues to render a qualified opinion as a juror."

"Like what? And how do you determine which types of things are covered by this system and which are not?"

"Well, there are a number of them. One is restaurant liability on food poisoning cases. It's rather scientific with regard to the toxins and food handling procedures, so that is one of the 'technical torts.' There are a few others. But many claims are heard by lay jurors such as slip and falls."

"Darin, you also mentioned the criminal laws here are more simple than the U.S. Is there much crime on Belle Isle?"

"No, virtually none."

"Why is that?"

"Well first of all, we have no poverty. Between our strong economy and charitable safety net, people don't need to steal or rob to put food on the table. Street crime is nil because we have so many people out walking at all times, including our cops, and the lighting is good. Also, being an island with limited access, gives us more security. If a crime is committed, say a break-in, then the monorail and bridge are secured and those are the only ways off the island, except to swim or take a boat. It works. You don't have to worry about safety here."

## CHAPTER 17

*Alexander Hamilton started the U.S. Treasury with nothing, and that was the closest our country has been to being even.*

*-Will Rogers*

## TREASURY and BANKING

The sandwiches finished, the two headed back out the front of the service center building and walked to the east to the next structure. Red reclaimed brick walls topped with a slate roof gave it an older look. It had a small sign in front that said, "Belle Isle Treasury."

Inside it looked like a U.S. bank. A meeting of five people was being conducted in a glass walled room. Two people were helping customers and several offices lined the exterior walls.

Darin pointed to the conference room. "These are the managers and accounting people who run the Treasury here. Belle Isle has a treasury like most larger countries. We toyed with the idea initially of using the U.S. dollar and in fact did so for our first few years, but the deficits of the U.S. and the ensuing inflation was disruptive to us. The value of our dollar denominated assets was falling and the European debt crisis concerned us. So we decided to cut ourselves loose from the U.S. dollar and start our own currency. As you know, it is called a Rand. We designate it by an "R" with a vertical line through it, much like the U.S. dollar is an 'S' with a vertical line. But since the alphabet characters don't have that particular one, we use 'R$' in our typed communications. We named it after Ayn Rand, the author of 'Atlas Shrugged' and 'Fountainhead.' She was a Libertarian whose views generally reflect ours. I know, I'm not supposed to use labels! She is on our R$100 bill, while we have some of the Austrian economists' pictures on other denominations — Hayek and Von Mises among them.

"When we first went with our own currency, we pegged it at par with the U.S. dollar, but our currency, unlike the dollar, has suffered no loss of value, in fact, we picked up a little, so our R$ today is equivalent in purchasing power to the 2012 U.S. Dollars. For example, a cup of specialty coffee here costs about R$3, which is what it cost in the U.S. back in 2012. Today in the U.S. that same cup of coffee costs $10 to $12.

"We have a contract with a private mint to do our currency printing and coin minting, but most transactions are done electronically. Another thing we have done is to try to back up our currency 100% with a basket of commodities. We initially started off with only gold. Our initial goal was to have at least 20 percent of the outstanding currency backed by gold, but have since added other commodities to the mix — silver, copper, oil and food contract rights and some stable foreign currencies among them. We have tried to create a mix which helps reduce the reliance on any one item. We are now nearly 100 percent backed by something of real value."

"So I could turn in a Rand for a barrel of oil?" Joe asked.

"Well, a Rand wouldn't buy you a full barrel. But you could turn in let's say a thousand Rand and receive in exchange a contract for delivery of about 10 barrels of oil which is fully assignable. In other words you could trade that contract for something else of value, say U.S. dollars or a fine dinner for 20 people."

"So how did you go from partial backing to 100 percent backing of the Rand?"

"Through our land sales, running surpluses and the requirement that new immigrant citizens made a contribution of initial capital."

"So the Rand must be well accepted, backed by gold and oil and so forth."

"Absolutely. You know the saying 'it's as good as gold.' We like to say 'it's better than gold!'" Darin smiled. Joe just shook his head.

Darin continued, "We have a currency board that is made up of five knowledgeable currency experts. They rotate in from the financial institutions and are appointed by the President and approved by the Council. Their clear mission is to maintain integrity of transactions and to keep the Rand strong and stable."

"Are there any banks on Belle Isle?"

"Of course. We have three banks. One is a community type bank owned by Belle Isle citizens. It's called First Bank and is free standing and located in the retail area. The other two are international — J.P. Morgan Chase and Credit Suisse and they're more office type operations in the Financial Center.  The big banks handle the bulk of the international transactions."


"Do you have government insurance or oversight on your banks?"


"No.  First Bank, being rather small, buys insurance from Lloyds to protect its depositors and Lloyds does the oversight of the loans and books.  That gives the depositors comfort. And if Lloyds starts charging too much or isn't giving service, First Bank can shop around in the world market and find a replacement.  U.S. banks can't do that with the FDIC — poor bastards!"

## CHAPTER 18

*It has been said that politics is the second oldest profession. I have learned that it bears a striking resemblance to the first.*

*-Ronald Reagan*


## YURI SERVENKOV


They headed outside again, boarded the monorail and got off at the financial center.


The financial center was actually a collection of office buildings, all connected by internal walkways and skyways.  The monorail platform overlooked the main atrium lobby.


The floor was a beige Trani marble with a central Port'Oro marble inset upon which a large walnut sheathed flower box was installed.  The day's freshly cut arrangement of roses and day lilies filled the flower box.  Brushed chrome elevator doors and trim turned the ceiling corner and transitioned into a large light fixture, suspended by chrome cables from the lobby ceiling.


Below them, people were entering and exiting through the main doors, which were secured in a fully open position.  Some were dressed in summer business suits, others in casual dress and even some in shorts.  There was a faint hint of the freshness of the river in the lobby.  Darin and Joe rode the escalator down to the lobby and proceeded to the elevator bank marked "25-48."

They got off on the 44th floor, turned right and faced an imposing corporate monument sign with large gold letters laid over a travertine marble wall that said, "Levy and Servenkov Capital Group."

Darin approached the receptionist. "I'm here to meet with Mr. Servenkov. My name is Darin Fraser, he's expecting me".

"Yes Mr. Fraser, one moment please. Please have a seat."

To the right of the reception desk was a lobby with full length windows overlooking the Belle Isle bridge. Beyond it, the sun sparkled off the Renaissance Center. Darin thought to himself that the name was now appropriate — just three generations later than Henry Ford II anticipated. Turning to the right, on the wall was a large video screen with a business reporter talking about the Asian stock market while a ticker scrolled below him.

"Darin, my dear friend, how are you?" A man dressed in a beige summer suit with an open collar was striding across the lobby with open arms and a large grin. He appeared to be in his mid-40's, was shorter than Darin by a good six inches and carried an extra 20 pounds over what his doctor probably wanted.

"It has been too long and I am so glad you have come by to visit." They hugged, then Darin introduced Joe and Yuri Servenkov, partner in Levy and Servenkov.

Yuri motioned them to follow him and he carded through two sets of security doors and down a long hallway. His office was impressive by most any standards. Joe thought it must be 30 x 40 feet, a corner office with two window views. One view was of the villages of Detroit, surrounded by small tracts of forests and many well cultivated farms and greenhouses. The other view was the river to the west, dominated by the Ren Center and the two bridges connecting the U.S. and Canada. Yuri's desk faced away from the views. It focused on an array of video screens; Joe counted eight, which had various stock and investment programs running. Behind Yuri's desk was a credenza with a collection of photos of Yuri with various people, most of them well known. Joe recognized four U.S. presidents, a Russian prime minister and a number of European heads of state. He didn't see any family photos and Joe speculated Yuri was unmarried.

On the far side of the office was a conference table with seating for 10. Decorating the walls were pictures of various investments the firm had made. They were quite varied. Some office buildings, a residential community the size of a small city, a research park filled the smaller wall, which seemed dedicated to real estate. On the longer wall, pictures of public utilities dominated. Several micro-nuclear electric power plants, a water treatment plant and a large number of micro-sewage treatment plants pictures were framed. Joe noted the Belle Isle utilities were among them, photographed from the air with the distinctive river in the background.

The three of them sat at the conference table as an assistant brought them glasses of Italian sparkling water with limes.

Yuri opened: "So Darin, I understand from your message your friend Joe is here from Syria to learn more about our wonderful island. What can I show Joe today?"

Darin responded: "Yuri, I'm sure Joe would like a tour of your offices, but more importantly I think he would be interested in learning more about you and your business and why you located it here on Belle Isle."

Yuri smiled at Joe, "You have a good amount of time? The story is not short!"

Joe interjected, "Yuri, the chairs are comfortable, the drinks are cold, the view is great. I couldn't ask for a better place to hear a long story. But I am still suffering from jet lag, so forgive me if at times I listen while examining my eyelids."

"Well Dr. Joe, I will just have to make it both interesting and short. My parents were born in Russia and came to this country before I was born. My father was a doctor in Russia but became very frustrated with the medical system there — it was still a throwback to the Soviet system and didn't reward their doctors very well. They settled near New York City and my father established a practice. I went to N.Y.U. and got a degree in political science and then an M.B.A. from Harvard. After graduation, I looked for job opportunities in the business and investment fields and researched carefully where the best business environments might be. New York of course has historically been the financial and business center for the U.S. and I was right there. But its tax rates and living costs were very high and it seemed to have lost some of its entrepreneurial zeal. I even researched Michigan, but even though Michigan's taxes weren't bad, its labor-dominated business policies inhibited doing anything creative, so I scratched it from my list too. But one thing did pop out of my Michigan investigation that directly affected my career path.

"Through a friend of my father, I arranged a meeting with the managing partner of a large venture capital fund in Michigan, just to pick his brain and get advice on what I should do with my life. He was helpful and in the course of our discussion, he told me an interesting story. His investment fund had taken a large position in an aerospace firm based in Phoenix, Arizona, and he was given a seat on the board of directors of this company. They were a supplier to Boeing, Airbus Industries, Embraer, Cessna and others, making precision products such as landing gear actuating assemblies.

"Well, this Michigan person, the new board member, was attending a quarterly board meeting in Phoenix and the management was giving their status report to the board. I guess it wasn't a good picture. The company was behind in its deliveries. It was having trouble hiring enough skilled tradespeople such as tool and die workers, machinists, precision welders and engineers to meet its requirements. Well, our Michigan investor raised his hand and said, 'Pardon me, Mr. Chairman, but I suggest we look at opening a plant in Southeastern Michigan. The Detroit area has an abundance of those talents as the auto industry has significantly downsized and skilled people are looking for work.' The Chairman removed his glasses and after a long pause looked our Michigan guy in the face and declared 'Michigan! The home of the communist UAW? You've got to be kidding. The business climate in Russia is better than Michigan!' That was the end of the discussion.

"I of course was shocked when this person told me the story, but it gave me an idea. I speak fluent Russian. I have a business degree from one of the top business schools in the U.S. And if it is true Russia has a 'better' business climate, perhaps I should check it out. So I did. First thing I saw was the Russian business income tax was only 20%, no capital gains tax, and personal income tax was a flat 13%, so I knew I was on the right path to finding a growing economy and more opportunities. I made several trips to Russia and was helped by my parents' relatives who remained. I soon found a position with a Russian oil and gas company that valued my business background and English skills, as many of the exploration engineering companies came from the U.K. and the U.S. My positions and pay quickly increased and within five years I headed up a region in Russia which was about 45% of our total production. I had more money than I knew what to do with and had lavish apartments in Moscow and London, and I spent considerable time in both.

"But then things became what one might call 'unraveled.' The company I worked for was privately owned. A Russian in his 40's and his family were the owners and I was always amazed on how we were able to get these valuable leases on great production areas in Russia. I was not involved in the lease bidding at all; we gave advice to the procurement people on what our chances were in being successful in finding oil and gas in a certain area so they could bid accordingly. And when we signed a lease, then it was handed over to us to find the oil and gas, but again we never did the bidding or negotiation.

"Well, one day, the FSB, they're the federal police, raided our Moscow offices and arrested our owner and confiscated all kinds of computers and records. Also a number of top management people were arrested and taken away. Thankfully, I was in London at the time. Apparently what had happened was the owner and the procurement department had been bribing for quite some time the Russian government officials who were in charge of the lease contract awards. An Asian competitor had upped the ante, which the Russians invited my owner to match. He said no in a not so nice way, so they shut him down, charged him with tax evasion and he is now in prison and the state took over the business and sold the assets off to the Asians.

"Me, I never went back to Russia. I couldn't get a clear answer as to whether I would be arrested and it didn't matter as I had no job there anyway.

"I headed back to New York and put feelers out. I got a job doing research work for a hedge fund managed by Levy and Levy. It involved both taking short positions at times on companies we felt were overvalued but also investing long in opportunities where the product idea and the management were strong. I started doing more of the latter and focused on the public utility side, particularly on new technology related to electric power, gas generation and transmission, and water and sewer systems. My timing was good as most communities were serviced by old technology and publicly managed systems, which were inefficient. Gas, electric and particularly water and sewer rates were rising each year, well in excess of inflation. So we got wind of some university research on small delivery platforms that actually were quite efficient as they minimized the transmission costs. We put some business people on the idea, they invested in the technology, sold the idea of privatization to the communities and started building these micro-utility operations. We even have one here. It's a 125 megawatt nuclear facility, which not only handles Belle Isle but we sell the excess to the U.S. and Canadian grids. It's highly efficient. So we provided the capital and it worked out well for everyone. The Levy partners were very impressed and when the New York investment crowd got wind of Belle Isle and decided to back it, Levy asked if I would like to establish an operation on Belle Isle and take an equal partnership with them in the company. They liked Belle Isle because it was central in the U.S. and we could investigate our investment opportunities more readily. When I heard there would be no tax on income and the philosophy of the island would be limited government, I said, or rather shouted 'YES!' So here I am."


Joe broke in, "So has it met your expectations? And do you ever get island fever?"


Yuri smiled. "Two questions. To the first, absolutely. There's an energy and confidence here I have never seen anywhere else. It's liberating to live here. This is truly the land of unlimited opportunity. To the second question, hardly. First of all, I am on the road about two days a week. For example, next week I will be in Palo Alto, Los Angeles, Fargo and Wichita on site visits and meeting management. I leave early Monday morning and am back here Tuesday night. Because of private aviation, I have only one night in a hotel as I visit four companies spread all over. Wednesday I'm going to a Tigers game in Detroit with a friend and we're going to have an early dinner in downtown Detroit. Thursday I plan to get caught up on my email and paperwork at the office. Friday, I'm attending a play at the Performing Arts Center here on the Island. Saturday and Sunday are the Gold Cup hydroplane races and that weekend is just nuts with all kinds of festivities and parties. I'll be watching the races themselves on my boat at the Detroit Yacht Club here on Belle Isle. There's plenty to do here. You know, rather than island fever, whenever I'm away, I miss this place because it is so cool!" Yuri drew out the cool with a big "ooooo."

"Darin and I used to go to the Detroit Yacht Club every summer to watch the hydroplane races from the end of their dock, when we were in high school and college," Joe said. "Darin's Dad would get us tickets. It was very cool. I think the Air Force jet doing its flight show right above our heads was as exciting as the boat races."

"Well, stick around until next weekend and you can be my guest on my boat to see it again."

"I wish I could. I'm afraid I can't stay that long."

"I'm sorry. I wish you could too. We have a lot of fun. Here on Belle Isle, we work hard and play a lot too and respect both."

They finished their drinks and Yuri gave them an office tour. Levy and Servenkov had the entire floor. Investment managers had window offices while the researchers had cubicles in the interior. Joe estimated the size at about 50 offices and workstations. One large room was for the day traders, its walls covered with various video feeds and non-stop scrolling tickers. There were four traders hunched over their computers, while a fifth was napping on a day bed, with his PDA lying on his chest to waken him if any programmed stops were hit.

The tour over, Darin and Joe thanked their host and headed for the elevator. They got off at the monorail level; Darin headed back to his office and Joe to the Four Seasons for an afternoon nap, armed with Darin's address in the residential district for their 7 p.m. dinner.

## CHAPTER 19

*One man with courage is a majority.*

*-Thomas Jefferson*


## DARIN'S DINNER


Joe had no problem finding Darin's condo. His PDA gave walking turn-by-turn instructions, but Joe felt as if he were in a European village with narrow streets and winding alleys. The streets were barely wide enough to handle emergency vehicles but were fine for pedestrians. Some were constructed of large polished gray cobbles, others were some combination of brick and stone. Attractive wrought iron street lamps were spaced along the walkways but didn't have electric bulbs; Joe wondered if they could be real gas lamps. He would have to ask Darin.


A doorman greeted Joe at 33 Rue de Rose. Holding the door open, he asked Joe whom he was visiting. The doorman responded with what Joe surmised was a British or Bermudian accent, "Ah, yes. You must be Dr. Sharif. Mr. Fraser is expecting you. The elevator bank is to your right. Take it to the 25th floor and exit to your right and go to the end of the hall. Have a wonderful dinner."


Finding the elevator, Joe took it to the 25th floor, turned right as instructed and after passing two doors, he was greeted by Darin standing in the doorway.


"Robert called me and said you were on your way. Welcome!"

Darin's office may have been austere, but his home was not. Not that it was huge, it was just super cool.

The condo had a clean modern feel with touches of natural materials. Italian grey stone pavers at the entry transitioned into a light oak floor of the Great Room. The ceiling was also the same light oak. Opposite the entry was a large fireplace with a chimney that reached to the 10' ceiling. Both the fireplace trim and chimney matched the stone pavers of the entry. On the walls were paintings and pictures Darin had acquired in Asia. Individual light fixtures resembling inverted snow cones hung from a serpentine chrome track lighting base.

Darin poured Joe some Pellegrino and they settled themselves in chairs on the balcony overlooking the river on the Detroit side. Below them were some families packing up from their day at the beach. To the west near the bridge, a large stucco building with a Spanish influence was girded by scaffolding.

Darin followed Joe's gaze. "That's the Detroit Boat Club restoration. The Boat Club was closed years ago, before the turn of the century and has really been run down. But it never got demolished and we decided to let it be. Well, the Detroit Yacht Club, which never closed, had become so successful and the waiting list for membership was so long, that a group from the wait list got together and bought the old Boat Club and is now fixing it up. They are keeping the original feel and décor, just the mechanical, electrical, energy and technology systems are being upgraded. When they finish, it will be something. They're tearing out all the old dock and putting new ones in, with some docks accommodating 100' yachts. I hear the DYC members are a little jealous."

"Do you get boats that big here?"

"Yes, we do. This area is starting to be a jumping off spot for yachts touring the Great Lakes. They come from Florida mainly; they winter down there and summer up here. They like to explore the North Channel and also do Charlevoix, Harbor Springs, Mackinac Island, even Door County on the Wisconsin side of Lake Michigan. On Lake Huron, they spend weeks in Georgian Bay — it's endless cruising. Some even get up into Lake Superior. A couple of years ago, I went with Yuri on his boat and cruised the North Channel and Georgian Bay. I have *never* seen anything so beautiful. It compares with the Greek islands."

They were interrupted by a call from the doorman. Two more guests were on the elevator. Darin headed to the door and welcomed the new arrivals.

Dr. John Miller was a tall man of about 50, tanned and fit with a ruddy complexion, prominent nose and receding hairline. Thomas Williams was of African descent, average height and quite thin. Joe guessed him to be about 40 even though his hair was already peppered with grey.

Before they had a chance to settle, the doorman called again to announce a third guest. Hector Cabrera was on his way up.

Darin greeted Hector at the door and introduced him to Joe. Hector was of medium height, with thick dark hair. His skin was quite dark and sun wrinkled. It was hard to gauge his age- perhaps mid-40's.

Darin poked Hector in the shoulder, "No Hector time on dinner invites my man! Ya done OK this time."

Hector smiled and shook his head. He didn't reply.

Darin looked at Joe who had a quizzical look.

"Private joke. I'll explain later."

## CHAPTER 20

*People are beginning to realize that the apparatus of government is costly. But what they do not know is that the burden falls inevitably on them.*

-Frederic Bastiat

## HEALTH CARE

The men retreated back to the balcony where drinks were served.

"Joe, John heads up the Belle Isle Medical Center and I thought you might be interested in learning more about his facility. The Med Center specializes in the treatment of spinal cord injuries. That's about the limit of my knowledge although I do know we get patients from all over the world who come here for help. Tom is the President of Belle Isle and is serving his first term. Hector emigrated from Mexico and has a landscaping business here plus oversees a great charity."

The two doctors engaged in technical conversation about the methods employed by the Med Center. Darin had heard it many times before but still didn't understand much of what was covered — the use of olfactory ensheathing gia cells along with the discovery of drugs that are used to counteract growth inhibitory proteins, allowing axon cell regeneration to occur. He and his building design team had of course approved the exterior architecture of the Med Center, but what happened inside wasn't his forte. But he understood the basics of the health insurance and when the technical talk wound down, segued to that subject.

"John, describe for Joe how we deliver medical services and how it's paid for."

John stroked his chin and drained his drink.

"Long version or short?"

Darin replied, "Whatever you want, but let's talk about it over dinner."

They moved to the dinner table and the waiter served the first course — a Moroccan chickpea soup.

"Well first the historical basis," John said.

"We all know what happened in the health care systems of our neighbors. In the U.S., they had excellent care but it was breaking the budgets and consumed an inordinate amount of the GDP, over 25%. Resources weren't allocated with any kind of emphasis on value. There was a disconnect between the patient and the provider. Insurance companies were in the middle and the patient was blind to the price of the product.

"In Canada, the government provided all the care but controlled spending by harsh rationing. If you were young and healthy, it worked fine but if you got really sick, you had to wait very long times for necessary care and a lot of people died who could have been saved. Many Canadians skipped across the border to the U.S. if they wanted to get urgent care.

"So we first established the ground rules. First of all, if a person had a congenital condition, then they would receive care. They would pay for it up to a reasonable limit based on their financial ability. So we as a society decided we were committed to spread the risk of that happening to one of our members. We spread that risk by paying through our taxes for the medical care required over and above what the patient could reasonably pay. And we're talking about citizens here. That is one of the benefits of citizenship.

"Now we're not necessarily talking about what was called 'pre-existing conditions.' Pre to what? If you were born with a defective heart, a new heart would be provided. But if you had poor eating habits and didn't exercise, were obese and developed Type II Diabetes as a result, then the support was limited. The patient is expected to do his or her part in creating good health. Second, the patient was fully apprised of the cost of treatment and had primary responsibility for paying for medical services. Now they could purchase insurance of course from private companies, but were encouraged to carry only catastrophic insurance to cover medical bills they couldn't afford. And companies didn't provide the insurance for their employees on a pre-tax basis, because we don't have any income taxes here. So people would form buying groups to get better rates by bulk buying.

"For example, teachers would band together to form a group, or accountants would do the same. And individuals would price before they buy. All our providers would issue price lists for things like office visits, surgeries, diagnostic testing, hospital stays, everything. This encouraged people to shop and therefore keep the pricing down. Doctors were judged based on metrics such as treatment cure rates and word of mouth. The free market would be allowed to function in the medical arena just like every other service. Information using complex statistical analyses has sprung up, some on a freeware basis, which rate the value propositions doctors and hospitals offer. Doctors work on keeping their prices down. And as we have a judicial system here that keeps medical malpractice insurance rates low, the prices tend to be lower. The insurance companies monitor the doctors closely on their malpractice claims paid, which effectively tended to weed out the incompetents."

Joe interrupted, "Yes, Darin and I sat in earlier today on a medical malpractice trial and he explained how that works. I really like the idea of claims being heard by medical professionals who can render knowledgeable judgments."

The soups were removed and replaced with an eggplant rollatini along with a sun-dried tomato salad, followed by lamb moussaka, sans lamb for Darin.

The two doctors continued their shop talk during dinner. John described to Joe some of the breakthroughs that had occurred in the last five years at the Belle Isle Medical Center on nerve reconstruction. Some patients who came in wheelchairs left walking on their own power.

# CHAPTER 21

*It is incumbent on every generation to pay its own debts as it goes.*

*-Thomas Jefferson*

## THE PRESIDENT

During the dessert of ginger-brandy cheesecake, the conversation turned from medicine to government. Darin initiated by asking President Tom Williams to describe for Joe what his day job was like and what duties he was expected to perform.

"Well, the charter is basically to manage and execute on the laws passed by the Council, which is our legislative branch. But unlike the President of the United States, I don't set or promote policy, with the exception that if the Council is contemplating something that cannot be effectively or efficiently performed, then I weigh in. For example, let's say they were considering passing a law prohibiting the chewing of gum in public, such as is the case in Singapore. I or my staff wouldn't say one way or the other whether we thought this was a good idea, but we would analyze and come up with a probable cost of enforcement, considering both the costs of police and the courts.

"It's a pretty straightforward position. I am a CPA by training and my primary job is to watch the Rands and keep spending from the inevitable 'creep' that seems to happen to many governments. We spend some time on compiling metrics of various types to make sure we are always in the top 10 percent of governments in terms of efficiency and thriftiness. The number of government employees per capita is a big one. Also, public expenditures per capita are another, although we have to factor out some of the expenses we have here such as heated streets and the monorail, which most other communities don't have. But when it comes to police, fire, courts, tax collections and the like, we excel in all those areas.

"A third metric is public expenditures as a percentage of GDP. Did you know that the U.S. was spending only 3 percent of GDP in 1929 and it rose in the Great Depression to 10. But in the 21$^{st}$ Century, it has often exceeded 20 percent. We don't want to repeat that mistake, so we have a goal of less than 10 percent and we stick to it."

"So how long do you serve and how did you get elected or appointed?" Joe asked.

Tom replied, "The term is four years, but subject to a recall process which *can* happen. If a petition comprising twenty five percent of the citizens is submitted that calls for a recall, then an election is scheduled within thirty days on the issue of recall. If a majority of the voters authorize the recall, then the president resigns immediately and the vice-president assumes the office on a temporary basis. A new election is scheduled 90 days out. The two top vote-getters then have a second run-off election 30 days later to elect the new president. The recalled president is eligible to run by the way."

"So your job is to keep the Island running, right?"

"It's somewhat more than that," Tom replied. "Yes, I oversee the public services group, which keeps the streets clean, the garbage picked up and the monorail running. We actually use private firms for those functions and bid it out each year. Same thing for the maintenance and janitorial of the publicly owned buildings. We have a procurement function, which handles those things. Police, fire, and taxation fall under my jurisdiction as does the maintenance and administration of the courts, legislature and jail. Of course, the judges themselves are independent as is the Legislature. So we have three branches of government similar to the U.S. and other countries — Legislative, Executive and Courts. We also have the anti-corruption group which is overseen jointly by the president and the legislature. We refer to it as the ACG."

## CHAPTER 22

*It will be of little avail to the people that the laws are made by men of their own choice if the laws be so volumi-nous that they cannot be read, or so incoherent that they cannot be understood----or undergo such incessant chang-es that no man who knows what the law is today can guess what it will be tomorrow.*

*-James Madison*

## LEGISLATORS

"How are the legislators elected and how long do they serve?"

"We have nine legislators. We call them Council Mem-bers. They have staggered terms of six years and elec-tions every two years. So each election, three are up for re-election. We have term limits, so nobody can serve more than two terms. Member are paid R$500 per month. That figure is based on what we estimate the av-erage hourly wage of an Islander is times the hours spent on Island matters. Being a Council Member is a part-time job. All of our Members have other activities, such as a full-time job or caring for their children or whatever. We definitely have citizen legislators."

President Williams continued, "The same recall mecha-nism applies to Council Members. If 25 percent of the citizens sign a recall petition, then a vote is held and a majority of the voters can recall the Member. If that happens, we have a special election to fill the position and a second election to decide among the two top vote

getters of the first. The new Member serves out the re-
maining term of the recalled Member."

Joe had questions. "You mentioned the anti-corruption
group. I assume they keep government clean, and you
mentioned there was joint oversight, but how does that
all work?"

"The ACG reports to the three Council Members who are
elected at large; one from each staggered term. The
fourth member is the president. So the four of us oversee the process. First, we have policies and procedures
to prevent corruption. We think it's much better to prevent it than to fix it after the fact. We use methods that
are used in banks and other businesses such as dual signatures, mandatory two consecutive week vacations, annual polygraph testing and a whistleblower call-in number, among others. Everyone in the public service is subject to these measures including the president and executive branch, the Council Members and the judges. We
have one full-time and two-part time people in the ACG."

Darin added, "There are two things that always sink any
ship — crime and corruption."

## CHAPTER 23

*When a man assumes a public trust he should consider himself a public property.*

*-Thomas Jefferson*


## JUDGES AND COURTS


"How about the judges, are they appointed or elected and how long do they serve?"


"The judges are appointed. In studying other countries and the United States, we found that pure democracy often doesn't work very well. Courtroom decisions are based on a complex set of facts and a plethora of information. For a citizen to analyze a judge's performance in arriving at his or her decisions requires both a legal background and a large commitment of time. We need our citizens to concentrate on building wealth for our society. The election of judges also tends to install so-called 'populist' judges, who are more likely to be redistributionists. So we appoint our judges. The judges are appointed by a commission comprised of four representatives selected by the Judges Appointment Commission and four representatives selected by the President. Half of the representatives are lawyers and half non-lawyers. The Minister of Justice chairs the commission and has a tie-breaking vote. They meet in private and deliberations are confidential. They recommend, with the consent of the President, judge candidates to the Commission for approval. The Commission approves with a majority vote in a public hearing. If the Council rejects the candidate, then the Council has to present an alternative candidate and the two candidates are voted upon by the citizens. If there are more than two candidates, the popular vote takes place in two elections, 30 days apart, with the second election being a run-off between the two top vote getters of the first election. Judges are also subject to recall by the citizens through a petition and voting process."

Darin broke in, "Joe, I know it sounds a little complicated, but it works well. The commission is in place for a full two-year period so appointing the commission doesn't take a lot of time. And let me tell you, you almost never see a political ad on TV with a judge!"

President Williams continued, "We have three courts. The Ordinary Court is the first level. It tries the criminal cases and hears the civil cases as well. We have two full-time judges and five part-time judges. The part-time judges are primarily semi-retired former full-time judges or former attorneys. We call the part-timers Substitute Judges. They all serve five-year staggered terms.

"The second level is the Court of Appeals. This has five judges and five Substitute Judges. All serve five-year terms, which are staggered. Any appeal is heard by the full contingent of five judges. These judges are part-time, on call. If anyone can't attend a hearing or has a conflict of interest, then a Substitute Judge serves, drawn by lot. The Court of Appeals will hear appeals from cases of the Ordinary Court, plus be the primary court for any legal actions brought against the decisions or works of the government. So let's say, the Council passes a law prohibiting chewing gum in public as is the law in Singapore, a private citizen could file an action in the Court of Appeals against this law.

"The third court is the Constitutional Court. This court has five judges, each appointed for a five-year term, again on a staggered basis. The Constitutional Court protects the rights of citizens accorded by the constitution and decides in matters of conflict between the executive branch and the council."

Darin interjected, "Share with Joe how judges are paid."

"Sure. Well as a bit of background, we wanted to improve upon the legal system typically seen in the U.S. where legal fees were astronomical. You know the saying 'only the lawyers get rich' and the length of time that was needed to reach a final decision could be years, and often was. So we take a business approach to the courts, particularly the Ordinary Courts, and set up a system of metrics. We measure how many hours in the court room; also we ask the attorneys for each side to keep track of their hours and submit that information to us on a confidential basis. We measure calendar days from first filing of the case to the ultimate decision by the judge. We also measure the appeal rate and how often Ordinary Court decisions were overturned by the Court of Appeals. We sort this information by type of case- felony criminal, misdemeanor, civil — technical or non-technical. For example divorce cases were one category on its own and of course non-technical. Medical malpractice cases are another in the technical area. After two years, we had some pretty interesting data and after five years some real solid information. We had one judge who used to start court at 10:00, take a one and a half hour lunch break and then knock off by 4:00 on a typical day. Well, when we first analyzed and published the data after two years, a petition drive mounted to recall this judge and he quickly resigned rather than face the election.

"The Ordinary Court primary judges are paid on a base plus incentive system, which is set by law. I don't recall the exact numbers but the base is of course the base salary and the commission is based on how many cases are decided according to a point system. For example, a misdemeanor is graded one point, felonies are graded between 10-20 points, depending on the charge. On the civil side, we have different classifications of both technical and non-technical cases with their points. At the end of each quarter, the points are added up for cases in which decisions have been rendered and the judge given extra compensation based on the points 'decided.' If a case is on appeal, then those points are withheld until the appeal process is decided. If the appeal goes against the judge, then the judge is given zero points for that case."


President Williams continued, "In the case of the Substitute Judges on the Ordinary Court, they are paid strictly on the point basis, they have no base pay. Most of them have other income and are doing it for extra money and to keep their hand in the game so to speak. We have found the system works great. You should see the looks on the judge's face when some bag of hot air attorney starts pontificating! And when the judge looks at his watch, you know it's time to wind it up."

# CHAPTER 24

*Why doesn't everyone leave everybody else the hell alone?*

*-Jimmy Durante*

## HECTOR CABRERA

Darin cut in, "Tom, speaking of winding it up, I know Joe is absolutely riveted by this legislator and judge stuff, but I want to tell Hector's story and the evening is not getting any younger.

Tom smiled. He knew once he got on a subject, he could be overly detailed and long winded, but it was in his CPA DNA. He relinquished the chair to Darin.

Darin turned to Joe, "Well the story starts about 15 years ago. I was on a mission trip to the Baja area of Mexico, to a town called Vicente Guerrero. It's about a day's drive south of Tijuana. A group of us were taking the week off between Christmas and New Years to build a house for a poor family. The house was very simple — built out of block, it had two sleeping rooms and a living room. No plumbing or electricity. It was wired for electricity but there was no service to the area. On the so-called plumbing, we dug a separate hole in the back and built an outhouse over it.

"Hector and his wife and two young children were going to live in the house when it was done. Until then, they were living nearby with her aunt sleeping on blankets on a dirt floor. So this was quite an upgrade. Concrete floor, actual beds — big step up.

"Hector had some construction skills. He could swing a hammer and could speak a little English and was very willing to help. We were amazed how hard he worked. He would be already working when we showed up in the morning and believe me, we showed up early. And he worked until dark, then insisted we go back to our motel while he cleaned up and put away the tools and building materials.

"We were there a week and I got talking with Hector and told him about Belle Isle; how it translated in French to 'Beautiful Island' and how it *was* beautiful, surrounded by clean fresh water. How the streets were clean and paved with beautiful bricks and the buildings stretched to the sky in their gleaming splendor. How the magic train went around the island above the peoples' heads. I could see I had Hector's attention.

"Then I told Hector about the people. How we had no crime. That everyone had a job or a role on the island. That we respected everyone's right to be the best they could be. That we treated everyone with respect - there were no majorities or minorities, no classes, no divisions among us, that everyone was rich in spirit. That we were truly the land of unlimited opportunity. Hector didn't understand that term in English so I had to make a stab at it in Spanish. 'Oportunidad sin limite.' Hector's eyes narrowed at me and said, 'es lo verdad?' 'Is this true?' I replied that it was."

Darin looked over at Hector and said, "Hector, what happened next?"

Hector's eyes were moist and he remained silent. Darin was sorry he had embarrassed his friend as Hector composed himself. He hadn't meant to.

Hector finally replied, "I'm sorry. That was a difficult time for me. I was happy over having this new house built for me and my family, but after Darin told me about Belle Isle that day, I knew more than anything else in the world, I wanted to live there. In my mind, the streets were paved with gold. So I asked Darin if I could move to Belle Isle. Darin told me most new citizens had to bring a lot of money with them, but there were exceptions. Exceptions had to make the case why they should be allowed to become a citizen. Exceptions also had to have a sponsor who was already a citizen. I asked Darin if he would be my sponsor. Darin said he would consider it, but what would I, Hector, contribute to the island, he asked. I told him I had skills with plants and flowers and would make Belle Isle, with all its water, even more beautiful than it already was. All I asked was for the opportunity to show him. I must have done a good job with my convincing Darin because here I am!"

Darin put his hand on Hector's arm, "it wasn't quite as simple as that. Hector wrote an essay with my help explaining why he wanted so much to live in a city where the core values of liberty, freedom, beauty, respect for others, unlimited opportunity and hard work were promoted. Where government stayed out of the way. I flew Hector up for an interview before the board. He was very nervous and his English didn't come across so well. The board granted him approval, subject to his English improving and having a job lined up here. He did both and moved here about six months later.

"After Hector and his family moved here, he worked for the company that had the trash removal contract with Belle Isle. He did that for over two years. It was a tough job. The trash removal takes place between 3 a.m. and 7 a.m., because of the vehicle restrictions. So he would get home about 10 in the morning after taking the trash to a land fill in Michigan, get some sleep, then study local horticulture. Hector had all kinds of plants and flowers he would grow in his small plot in one of our parks that he leased for a small amount from the city. Hector experimented with different techniques and soils, seeds, fertilizer and arrangements. Over a couple of years, he had become an expert in not only designing, but building gardens of exceptional beauty.

"Hector got noticed by some Islanders who hired him to do their gardens. So Hector moved trash at night and planted and tended gardens in the day. He worked hard and made enough money to even pay full fare for one of his girl's schooling. The other remained on scholarship for a few more years.

"After about three years on Belle Isle, Hector was able to successfully bid on the plantings and flowers for one of our parks — Parc de Leon. We have five parks on the island and bid them out every two years. It was a design/build project and Hector did a wonderful job. This gave him some extra points when bidding on other parks. He now has Parc de Leon and the Casino park. The Casino park is the one next to the Hotel Four Seasons and is our monument park, so that one is a big deal.

"Well, between his two big park contracts and the private homeowners business, Hector has quite an operation going. In fact, he is the largest summertime employer on the island. How many people do you have working for you now?" Darin turned to Hector.

"About 160."

"How many are kids?"

"All but five."

Darin continued, "So Hector has about 155 kids working for him. During the summer they all show up at Parc de Leon at 8:50 in the morning. He and his foremen give them the tools and instructions and send them to the parks, businesses and homes for their work day."

Joe asked, "Why 8:50 rather than 9:00?"

Hector said, "I tell them you start work at 9:00, but if you're not 10 minutes early, you're late. The first timers look at me like I'm crazy, but they soon learn about 'Hector Time' — if you're not early you're late. And if they aren't there when we leave for the job, there's no catching up. We send them home."

Darin jumped in, "Since almost all the kids on the island work for Hector at some point they go home and tell their parents about Hector Time, *everyone* started to use the term 'Hector Time.' It's become so much a part of our culture that most times, people are a little early for their appointments. Nobody waits. Someday we need to build a big clock tower downtown where the clock is 10 minutes fast with a picture of Hector on its face!"

Hector flushed deep red, despite his tan. "I am a lucky man."

Joe asked, "Hector, I hope you don't mind me being nosy, but what do you pay these kids? Do you pay minimum wage?"

"I pay them whatever their work is worth. Some get a little more than others."

Darin added, "Joe, there is no minimum wage here. Minimum wage laws foster unemployment, particularly among young people. We follow Singapore's example on this. The parents of these kids, who are almost always well off, are happy their kids are working, learning Hector Time and other good work habits and making their own money. Whatever they make is secondary."

Hector smiled, "Yes and I tell the kids — 'you make it, you take it'. Nothing comes out of their paycheck. No taxes."

Darin turned to his friend, "Hector, tell Joe about the charity you and Herbert started."

Hector brightened. "Well, years ago, I was taking a cab in Detroit from the Transportation Center to downtown and the cab driver, this black guy, asked where I was from. I told him I was originally from Mexico so he tried out some Spanish on me. His Spanish was so-so but he really wanted to improve. We hit it off and whenever I came over to Detroit, I would call ahead and ask for him by name to be my driver. One thing led to another and we would have a coffee and a bite after he got off work, if our schedules worked out. Well, I learned he had quite an interesting past — in some ways like mine. He grew up in Oak Park. As a young black man, he hung out with the wrong people, got involved with a gang, ended up doing drugs and selling them. He shot another gang member and spent five years in prison. When he got out, he was running numbers and driving a cab when I met him. I told him about me coming to Belle Isle and what it meant to me, how I was working two jobs and making something of my life. I guess I gave him some hope. He was a real bright guy with numbers. I told him he should go back to school and learn business. He got into Wayne State and put himself through school. I loaned him some money along the way. He went on to get his graduate degree in Accounting and then became a CPA."

Darin interrupted, "Joe, you met him this morning. That was Herbert Watson, who heads up our accounting for the Service Center."

Joe was surprised. "That's quite a story. I guess it shows it's never too late to get your life in order."

Hector continued, "Herbert really wanted to work on Belle Isle. He got a job in our tax department here working on valuations. Did that for five years and then applied for citizenship. I sponsored him."

Joe asked, "You mean Belle Isle actually granted citizenship to a convicted felon with a drug history?"

Tom answered, "It certainly is an exception to give citizen status to someone with that kind of past, but it can and does happen. We are always looking through the windshield, not the rear view mirror. Everyone should have hope for a better future. It's up to them to make it better."

Joe queried, "So Hector, tell me about the charity you and Herbert have going."

"I was getting to that. Got a little sidetracked with Herbert. Herbert and I formed a group called 'Seeds of Detroit.' We take people who share our beliefs in self-reliance and hard work. They work and live on Belle Isle for about two years so the island culture becomes a part of them. The Belle Isle core principles of limited government, appreciation of beauty and respect for all human beings becomes part of their beliefs. During that time they take classes on leadership and business. After two years, they go back to Detroit and use their skills to create a better world on the other side of the river."

"Has it been successful?"

"Very successful. One of our graduates — we call them 'seeders' started a program where he trains 'horticultural technicians.' They grow flowers and unusual vegetables on plots of urban farms that separate the Detroit communities. These horticultural technicians grow their products on pieces of land that they rent from the company for a nominal amount, then over time purchase their property using the profits from the sales of their flowers and vegetables. Along with other people like themselves, they form cooperatives to help buy fertilizers they need and then to sell their products on a collective basis. Another seeder teaches a class in Belle Isle civics to students at the University of Detroit Mercy. I hear it's always full."

# CHAPTER 25

*As a taxpayer, you are required to be fully in compliance with the United States Tax Code, which is currently the size and weight of the Budweiser Clydesdales.*

*-Dave Barry*

## THE VIEW

Joe looked at his watch, "I know it's not even 11:00, but I'm still on Damascus time somewhat, so I'm not going to last much longer."

Darin stood up, "Joe, before you go, how about a little espresso on the balcony?  You gotta see the view."

Darin led the way through a patio door to a second balcony off the great room.  The floor of the balcony was tiled in grey stone, the walls were a white stucco.  Gaslight sconces produced a soft flickering glow.  Darin turned the sconces to a low setting and the four men leaned against the rail.  Joe was reminded to ask Darin about the street lights on Rue de Rose.

"Yes, they are real gas lights.  Whenever we can we try to the use the real thing.  Truth in architecture, truth in government.  It's all connected."

They were facing south.  To the right was downtown Windsor, whose dominate landmark was the Windsor Casino.  Pairs of headlights in motion defined the streets and the fact the city was still alive at that hour.  Straight ahead in the distance white and green lights alternately flashed.


"That's Windsor airport. Quite a view isn't it? I never get tired of it, especially on a warm summer's night. Although I have to tell you, with the infrared heaters going, the spring and fall evenings are terrific too."


A large rectangular glass table with six chairs was centered on the balcony. The five men took the chairs with the views and a server appeared with a tray of espresso cups, port glasses and brandy snifters. A return trip brought a bottle of Sandeman 20 year old port and Remy Martin V cognac, along with a humidor filled with fine cigars. Joe took a cup of espresso, passed on the cigar as did John and Hector. Darin and Tom took a port, John a cognac and Hector a brandy.


Darin handed a cutter to Tom and to one in particular said, "Our good president prefers a Cuban Cohiba but I'm partial to a Padron 1926 Anniversaire Series. I don't think the Cubans ever really got their quality back, even after Castro died. But Tom and I have debates on that subject."


Drinks and cigars going, Darin reached under the table, pressed a button and the table came to life. It was actually a TV screen. Joe estimated it must be about 60" by 48." Displayed was an aerial map image of the surrounding area around Belle Isle. A portion of Lake St. Clair, the Detroit River past the Ambassador bridge, Detroit and Windsor were marked in faint outlines. A building on Belle Isle, apparently Darin's condo, was marked in a slightly bolder outline. But dominating the screen were small aircraft symbols moving at measured paces in all different directions.  Next to each airplane were various numbers.  Joe looked in amazement at the table.   Next to an air symbol were the characters "BA22," "275," "42," and "DTW-HEA-11:25."  Joe looked to the south in the general direction indicated by the symbol and saw a plane's strobe light as it moved from right to left.

Joe asked Darin, "Is that plane off in the distance the one on the screen here?"  Joe pointed to an airplane symbol moving toward the east.

Darin took a pen like object that had been lying on the table and pointed it at the blinking light in the south sky.  Immediately on the table screen, the "BA 22" plane symbol blossomed into an image twice the size and brightness as the others.

"Yep, that's it.  That's British Airways Flight #22 going from Detroit to London Heathrow.  Its ground speed is 275 knots and it's climbing through 4,200' and estimated to arrive Heathrow at 11:25 Greenwich Mean Time.  This pointer has a directional signal picked up by a device connected to the screen, so it knows where I'm pointing it and identifies the object on the map."

"Amazing stuff."

"Well it's fun to play with.  Did you ever look up at the night sky, see a plane and wonder where it was going?  I don't need to wonder.  I just point at it and it tells me pretty much everything I want to know.  This screen is hooked up to a system called Flight-Tracker and every airplane that is on a flight plan in the world is on here."

Darin touched a control on the screen and instantly the entire United States was in view, with hundreds of tiny white dots moving in all directions, resembling a swarm of white bees.  He touched another control the view shifted to Japan and Asia, with even more white bees flying randomly.

"I have another program on here that tracks ships.  Same thing.  See that light off there off in Lake St. Clair?"  Joe peered to the east through the glass balcony rail and saw a pair of lights, green on the left and red on the right.

Darin aimed the pointer and a boat icon flashed big with the name "Arthur Anderson" "Duluth-Cleveland."

While Darin and Tom smoked their cigars, Joe played with the pointer, aiming it at various planes in the sky and looking at the screen for the plane's information. Next week, he would be a spot on the screen.  He wondered if Darin would be out here looking for him.

The discussion about Belle Isle government was over, replaced by good espresso, good port, good cognac, good cigars, good friends and faraway places.  Below them the Detroit River seductively beckoned.

Darin mused, "You know, from right here, you can sail to anywhere in the world."

## CHAPTER 26

*Why is it that statists believe that if you tax cigarettes you will discourage smoking but if you tax work, risk-taking and capital formation, you will get a healthier economy?*

*-Larry Reed*

## THE LAST DAY

In the distance Joe was starting to make out the palm trees. Their tops were waving wildly in the wind, like magnets drawing him closer. Then the beach appeared. Its sands seemed endless. He was worried about grounding his sailboat as the waters shallowed. No time to do that after sailing for months from Belle Isle. He heard chimes in the distance. Could that be a warning bell indicating a reef?

The chimes grew louder and Joe opened his eyes. The sun was already up despite it being 7 a.m. He killed the chimes on the clock next to his bed and gazed at the ceiling, buying a few minutes before starting on the new day. It had been an incredible visit so far. He was amazed at what great things the human spirit could achieve, if allowed to be in a state of choice, rather than force. Free to succeed, free to fail. But most of all, free. Without failure, there can be no success.

He mused how happy people appeared to be on the streets. He wondered if they were happy in the winter, when the weather was cold and daylight was shorter. Joe thought the architecture and gas lights made the streets look enchanted last night. With heated streets and walks, he could see it might not be so bad in the winter.

Darin had done a great job, but of course he was first to admit he had plenty of help. He said he was a lucky guy.

Joe joined Darin on the outdoor patio area of the Four Seasons. They served meals outside starting April 1st and going through the end of October, aided by overhead infrared heaters. If the wind were to blow, there were Plexiglas curtains that could be lowered to protect the patrons. But this morning the temperature was 75 and the wind was calm. It was a great spot to watch the boats.

Darin ordered a vegetarian omelet while Joe munched on yogurt and granola. Darin shared the day's plans.

"It's impossible to show you everything. There's just too much, but today we'll hit the School/Worship District, the Sports District and more of the Entertainment District which includes the theater. Also, I think you might be interested in the Market and the Transportation Center."

"You're the tour guide. You lead, I follow!"

CHAPTER 27

*Inflation is as violent as a mugger, as frightening as an armed robber and as deadly as a hit man.*

*-Ronald Reagan*


## SCHOOL and WORSHIP DISTRICT


They exited the monorail at the platform marked School/Worship District. There was a commons area, much like a village green and on it were about a dozen buildings, all of varied design. Joe first saw a mosque, similar to ones in Syria, with a gleaming gold dome and minarets. Separated by only a hundred feet or so was a church constructed of stone topped by a bell tower. Brick walks meandered among the buildings connecting them with the monorail station. There was a reflecting pool in the middle of the commons with a pathway of grey stone pavers encircling it. The buildings were sprinkled around the perimeter of the pool. It reminded Joe somewhat of EPCOT Center at Disney World, by the way the buildings were located, but there was none of the amusement park fake façade feeling to it. These buildings were beautiful and they were real.


Walking around the pool to the left, they passed the church and came to a synagogue. It was generally traditional, although it had a few modern elements to its architecture. Darin explained how the various members of the synagogue argued as to whether it would be traditional or modern. As the Belle Isle Architectural and Planning Board had the final say, Darin was able to bring the decision to a conclusion, backed up by some of his Israeli friends who had worked on the Malaysia project with him.

Past the synagogue was a Roman Catholic church. The architecture was traditional, with some of the elements which reminded one of the Cathedral of Notre Dame in Paris. Darin explained that Belle Isle was going to be around for a very long time, so he didn't want any architecture that would become dated.

Other Protestant churches and a Hindu temple completed the circuit around the reflecting pool. All were quite different but done in traditional architectural styles.

Joe and Darin came to a walk made of stone that branched off to the east. About 200 feet past the last church they came to a three-story brick and stucco building with a stone façade. It had a crock tile roof and it reminded Joe of some of the buildings he had seen in Turkey on his travels there. Darin remarked that this was a kindergarten through eighth grade school and that it was privately owned. Over the front door engraved in stone was, "Belle Isle Junior Academy." Across the street was a similar building but done entirely in stone with a slate roof. Its monument sign was in front and said, "Belle Isle Senior Academy" and served the ninth through 12th grade classes.

Darin explained, "We have two K-12 schools on the island. Both are privately owned and operated. Up ahead is the second pair, which are named the 'Friedman Upper School' and 'Friedman Lower School.' The grade structure is the same K-8 for the lower school and 9-12 for the upper school. Over to the right is the football and soccer field that the schools share, and next to it is the basketball arena, again shared. They share it under a joint operating agreement. The schools work out their practice and game schedules well before the school year starts to avoid conflicts. The other sports facilities on the other side of the walk include a baseball diamond and an indoor hockey arena. Again they are shared."

"Which school owns these things?"

"Actually, neither. All the sports facilities are privately owned by organizations that were set up to be what we call 'donor led.' In the U.S., there are non-profits that are structured to attract donors because donations to them are income tax deductions. But here we have no income tax, so we don't have that advantage — if you call it that, but the donors are there just the same."

Joe pressed, "Well, why would they donate without the tax break?"

"Because they want to and it's a great cause. Most of the donors or their kids have used the facilities. It is a non-profit with a volunteer board, which oversees the operations. They charge expenses to the school users but it is very low. And the schools sell tickets to their games which brings in a little bit of revenue for the schools and pretty much covers what they have to pay for the facilities. We also have a few Red Wings and Lions practices here which are big draws and they raise funds from spectator sales. So, the schools really pay next to nothing for their use."

"So Darin, are there any public schools on Belle Isle?"

"No, only the two private schools."

"How much is the tuition?"

"It varies by grade and the two schools have slightly different pricing. I'm not totally up on it but I think the early grades are about R$8,000 and the high schools are about R$12,000."

"And these schools are for profit?"

"No, they're donor led non-profits"

"Why non-profit? I remember you telling me you encourage for-profits."

"We love for-profits, but the non-profit donor led model works well for schools. It makes fund-raising much easier and our citizens recognize the need for a well-educated populace."

"But that tuition is pretty expensive. How many people can afford it?"

"I hear 85 percent of the students are paying full fare. You have to remember, our citizens pay no income tax. They are well educated and they make very good money. The median household income here is over R$100,000 and they take it all home. Two kids in high school and one in grade school is really no problem for the typical family. Of the 15% who have scholarship assistance, they pay a percentage based upon their income and some other factors, but everyone pays something. The schools have very involved parents because all the parents are writing checks. There are no free rides. Remember, free is a four letter word starting with 'f'."

"How are the schools rated?"

"Very good. On par with Detroit Country Day, Cranbrook or U of D Jesuit. Many of our kids go to Ivy League schools or good west coast universities. These schools have adopted the 11 month school year convention, which gives them a leg up on the old agrarian-based system of 9 months. All the Friedman school graduates go on to college, much like Country Day students when we were there. But the Belle Isle schools have a somewhat different approach. If a graduate goes on to technical school, rather than college, that's fine. About 15 to 20 percent of the graduates go that route.

"Around the corner there, you can't see it from here, is the Belle Isle School of the Technical Arts. We call it Tech-Arts for short. There all kinds of skills are taught. We have skilled construction trades such as carpenters, plumbers and electricians, but also stone-cutting, fine masonry and plastering. It's said we have the finest skilled construction trades in North America coming out of here. It goes well with the need for those lost arts here on Belle Isle with our architectural goals and requirements. And with the revival of the Detroit region and its fine homes, there is a lot of work across the river as well. Tech-Arts has some terrific computer and communication technician classes and of course those jobs are in high demand. They also have horticulture training and many of those people are employed taking care of the many gardens we have here on the island. Another area of study is home management."

"What is home management?" By his tone of voice, Joe seemed doubtful.

"Well, back in the middle of the 20<sup>th</sup> century, co-ed colleges often had home economics classes, largely for women that would prepare them to be housewives and take care of the kids and the home. Home management is designed as a cross between being a traditional housewife, a butler, a chef and a business manager. It's a two-year program and a graduate does everything to manage and provide the service for the home. They prepare fine meals, not to New York chef standards, but good dining. They can do basic home repairs. They do the food shopping. They shop for clothes for the kids if needed. They know how to set the table correctly. They can mix drinks and be a server at home parties. They also take bids from outside contractors, prepare payment requests for the owner and keep the household books, including preparing the budget and producing financial statements. It's a large responsibility and the better home managers are well paid averaging about $R75,000 and some are north of $R100,000 per year. Somewhere about 10 percent of the households here have full-time home managers and another 25% have part timers."

"It sounds like a pretty good job."

"Exactly and you know, these people are respected. We all know who the best ones are and they are always getting offers to move. Some are like rock stars! We have a few families here who won't talk to one another because of a home manager was 'poached.' It's interesting."

They continued along the stone walk. It curved back around toward the monorail.

"I would give you a tour of the schools, but they're closed for the summer. From mid-June through August the kids are off, although the sports programs go year around. Many of our residents have summer places in northern Michigan or Ontario and go there for the summer."

Darin and Joe boarded the monorail at the School/Worship station. They switched trains at the Office station and boarded the next train for the Transportation Center.

## CHAPTER 28

*You can't get rid of poverty by giving people money.*

*-P.J. O'Rourke*


## TRANSPORTATION CENTER


The Transportation Center monorail was faster than the local and they soon crossed the Detroit River and arrived at a station marked "Transportation Center." Exiting through a pair of automatic double doors, an overhead sign showed "Ground Transportation" to the left and "Air Transportation" to the right. They followed the "Ground" sign and entered a lobby that had two rental car desks and behind it a "Zipcar" directional sign. Going past the rental car desks and turning to the right, they entered a parking deck filled with cars.


Darin motioned his hand over the deck filled with cars.


"These cars are mostly owned by Belle Isle residents. The deck is on Detroit property but on a 99-year lease with Belle Isle. If someone has a car here, they pay rent to the Transportation Center owner which is a private company but rates are approved by the Belle Isle legislature, according to the return on investment standard I talked about before. It works out to about R$150 per month per parking space.


"We also have a fleet of Zipcars here, for people who don't want to have the costs of ownership and parking or just have access to a second car. It is very popular. And of course, there is a line of cabs out front too.

"Joe, let's go check out the air terminal."

They turned around and headed toward the air transportation part of the building.  A desk with a sign above marked "Belle Isle Air" was manned by an attractive middle aged woman and an older distinguished man dressed in matching blue uniforms.

To their left was a ramp filled with airplanes, ranging in size from single engine propeller to larger twin engine corporate jets.  Across the ramp was a taxiway leading to a parallel runway, approximately aligned with the river.  On the other side of the runway were rows of hangars, a mix of small and corporate sized.  A control tower was midfield, dominating the view.

A business jet was on takeoff roll heading east to west.  They stopped and watched as it lifted off and made a left turn.  The sun mirrored off the lowered wing.

"Where do the planes go from here?"  Joe asked.

"Well, the runway is about 7,500' long so we have business jets that can take off and fly directly from here to all the major cities in Europe.  London, Paris, Rome, even Istanbul, Cairo and Tel Aviv.  Going west, Tokyo and Seoul requires a fuel stop.  So basically anywhere in the western world non-stop and anywhere in the world with one stop."

"How about Andrew's company plane?"

"Oh, it's strictly for the U.S. and has a shorter range. It can take six people and go to L.A. That's about it.

"We also have an active charter operation here for those companies that can't use a plane enough to justify owning one. Belle Isle Air has eight airplanes. Many of their customers are Detroit-based companies, not just Belle Islanders."

As they headed back toward the monorail, Darin and Joe passed a money exchange. It had exchange rates for many countries but in bold letters at the top of the chart was "Dollar-Rand." The rate posted was $3.28 Buy and $3.35 Sell.

Joe stopped and studied the rate board.

"Darin, you say the dollar and Rand were at parity about 20 years ago? Did the dollar really drop that much?"

"Compared to the Rand it did. All the major world currencies have suffered inflation, but the U.S. dollar has suffered more than most, since it was essentially delisted as the world's reserve currency in 2015. The U.S. ran such large deficits and the Federal Reserve started printing money like there was no tomorrow in an unsuccessful attempt to stimulate employment. But all it did was make investors lose confidence and flee the U.S., especially the Chinese, which made the problem worse.

"The problem with the Fed was it had two conflicting missions — a stable dollar and full employment. The politics of the matter and some bad leadership by the Fed Chairman and Board of Governors got them down the stimulus path, but it didn't work. All they did by throwing money into the system was to undermine the whole capitalist structure. The deficits were so huge, by the time they figured it out, it was too late. The U.S. had its bonds de-rated, which caused massive inflation for the U.S. citizens and dollar holders.

"Here, we took a different approach. Our goal has been and will always be zero inflation. That puts us in a very favored status by investors and we have no problem raising capital, which provides full employment."

They headed back to the monorail and were back in the Financial Center station after a six minute ride.

## CHAPTER 29

*Politics is the art of looking for trouble, finding it every-
where, diagnosing it incorrectly, and applying the wrong
remedies.*

*-Groucho Marx*

## MARKET

They used the stairs rather than the escalator. The sun
was bright. Rather than board the local monorail, Darin
and Joe walked north across the island to the open air
market. A stone arch emblazoned with the word, "Market," marked the entrance. Inside was row after row of
tables, most shielded by awnings. Farmers were hawking
fruits and vegetables, artisans their jewelry and a few
others were showing off their paintings. Joe saw a couple sizing up his and her sweatshirts with an outline of
the island on the front and a large "Belle Isle" below. After their purchase, the vendor took a picture of them
wearing their matching clothing.

It was about lunchtime and Darin suggested they eat at
the market. They could smell lamb cooking and stopped
at a gyro sandwich stall for Joe, while Darin bought a
veggie pita. Nearby was a fruit stand with tomatoes and
vegetables of all kinds.

"Where does this stuff come from?"

Darin replied, "Some are grown in Greater Detroit. There
are several orchards there. Others are grown farther
north. They get brought in every day in the early hours

during the time motorized vehicles are allowed, before 7 in the morning."

They found a bench open near the Market's perimeter and settled there to eat. Joe guessed the temperature must be close to 80. Although from where they were sitting there was no water view, the people watching was a good substitute. Tourists were wandering about, with cameras in one hand and kids in the other. They could have been from anywhere in the world. Joe played a mind game where he guessed their country of origin. A Swedish couple no doubt — both blonde. Another couple — he with a ruddy complexion and she had red hair. Must be a Brit married to an Irish lassie. A man with a dark complexion and a prominent nose, maybe Croatian? The game was basically idle curiosity and Joe never found out the actual origin. But it seemed there were many tourists and Joe heard many languages being spoken.

"Darin, you get a lot of tourists here? I mean other than people from Detroit area or Windsor."

"Many. We keep track. Belle Isle is a big tourist draw but it's not their only destination. They spend time in Detroit too. People see this both as an interesting social experiment and a fun place. What do you think?"

Joe chose his words carefully. "I think it is beyond interesting. What I see is the human spirit liberated and the result is amazing. I've been watching the people here carefully. It's sort of a combination of the energy of New York City with the friendliness of the Midwest. I've done quite a bit of travel all over the world but have never seen anything quite like this. I really think you have done something exceptional here."

"I've had help, believe me. Some of the best minds in the world have participated and often asked for little in return. I think what helped us is the original groundwork and vision of a society where government gets out of the way. We just need to protect the field from intruders and let the farmers grow their crops, so to speak."

The sun continued its slow journey toward the west as it warmed the market. Darin suggested they consider going to a play at the Performing Arts Center that evening, but Joe preferred to just have a leisurely dinner and take in the sights, sounds and smells of the island. It was going to be just too nice to be inside. They agreed to meet in the hotel bar at 7 p.m. and then go to dinner.

## CHAPTER 30

*Only a crisis — actual or perceived – produces real change. When that crisis occurs, the actions that are taken depend on the ideas that are lying around. That, I believe, is our basic function: to develop alternatives to existing policies, to keep them alive and available until the politically impossible becomes politically inevitable.*

-Milton Friedman

## CRONY CAPITALISM

Darin was already at the bar when Joe arrived. He looked lost in thought, staring at nothing in particular.

"Hey Darin, what's happening? You look too serious man, are you working on some new project?"

"No, I was just thinking about how much time has passed since we last saw each other. It's scary that it happened so quickly. I hope we do better keeping in touch going forward."

"I'm with you on that," Joe said. "Sometimes I think we get so wrapped up in our careers or the day-to-day stuff that we lose focus. Days turn into weeks, weeks into years, years into decades, decades into a lifetime. But you've made the most of it. It's just incredible to me what you've done here. You must be proud."

Darin continued to gaze at nothing. "Yes I am proud, but worried too. Proud that I could be a part of a movement that turned the tide from negativism and paternalism to freedom and economic liberty. But worried that we might slip backwards toward elitist so-called experts who know better than the rest of us, and letting those people make the rules. And you can bet that once the experts allow the camel's nose into the tent, the stampede of their capitalist cronies on their coat-tails soon follows."

"But I thought you were pro-capitalism. What are you saying?" Joe asked.

"I am pro-capitalism. But I am against those who in the name of capitalism use government to give themselves a monopoly or competitive advantage."

"What do you mean? Give me an example."

"Let me think." Darin paused for a bit then said, "Sure, I'll give you an example. I'm an architect, right? So I get involved in building specifications and codes. Companies that make fire suppression sprinkler heads, piping and valving have long been lobbying for mandatory inclusion of sprinkler systems in buildings. They do it by funding some study that purports to show that a sprinkled building saves lives. Now I personally don't think so. Smoke detectors, especially the latest generation, which detect a fire before there's even any flame, *do* save lives. Get 'em out of the building! By the time the sprinklers go off, it's pretty late in the game. I agree that often property damage is reduced by sprinklers, although in some cases I've seen some terrible damage from sprinklers going off accidently. But my point is, the people who are affected — the person paying for the building and the person living in the building are not consulted on what *they* prefer. The experts know better. No way! The experts are just working for people who are lining their own pockets. That's what I mean by crony capitalism. Of course, there are a million other examples. It's not quite hard corruption. Let's call it soft corruption, at least a conflict of interest. I once looked up the dictionary definition of 'corruption'. It was 'perversion of integrity.' That's pretty broad."


Darin's brow was furrowed and his passion was center stage. Joe had not seen this in Darin before.


"Whoa, let's go get some dinner. As a doctor, I'm diagnosing you with a sugar low!"


Darin looked over at Joe and smiled. "Yeah, I guess I get wound up. But you know, I see this as a war of sorts. People who sell their souls for a buck. They know what's right and wrong, but choose to look the other way. We must ever resist the tendency. I know it's as old as time, but the truly great societies have become great by rising above it. But let's go eat. We can talk over dinner."

## CHAPTER 31

*My reading of history convinces me most bad government results from too much government.*

*-Thomas Jefferson.*

## JOBS

Darin and Joe hopped on the monorail and headed east, getting off at one of the residential stops. Darin suggested they dine at a small bistro overlooking Blue Heron Lagoon called "Ten Tables." It was a favorite of the locals as they could walk a block or two in the morning for coffee and croissants without having to get on the monorail. In the evening, it specialized in exotic vegetarian dishes, making it a rather frequent dinner spot for Darin.

As they walked along the cobble street towards Ten Tables, Darin and Joe stopped to look at a building under construction. Four stories in height, the front was largely stone with some brick and stucco accents. The sides were stucco, accented by some artistry. Joe noticed some gargoyles on the front near the roofline. It reminded him of some buildings he had seen in Prague.

Two men were in conversation in the front yard. They noticed Darin and Joe and came over to introduce themselves. One appeared to be about 55 and the other around 30.

The older one opened with, "So how do you like it?"

Joe replied, "It's beautiful. It reminds me of Prague. Of the cities of the world I've visited, Prague is in my mind the most beautiful, but I have to say Belle Isle is giving it a run for its money. I'm visiting here and it is amazing."

"Thanks, but I can't take credit for the way it looks. I'm just the builder, not the architect. But we do take pride on how it comes out and we do our best to make sure our workmanship exceeds what the owner and the architect expect. Say, where're you from?"

"I live in Syria, but I was born and raised in the Detroit area. I'm visiting my friend here who lives on Belle Isle. He's giving me the full tour. By the way, I'm Joe Sharif and this is Darin Fraser."

"Joe and Darin, good to meet you. I'm Calvin Doakes and this is my son Claudio."

Joe could see the family resemblance. Both were good looking men of African descent and had the same eyes and noses, just Calvin had a sprinkle of grey hair.

Joe asked, "So Calvin, there sure seems to be a lot of construction around here, have you been a part of it?"

"Yes sir, I have. I got started here about 20 years ago, when Belle Isle got really going in a big way. I'm from Detroit and before Belle Isle came along, I didn't think there was any hope for me. I was on Section 8 and food stamps and any other government program I could find, but I just knew my life was going by. What was I going to be remembered for when I was gone? It really bothered me. Then Belle Isle was sold by the city to this group for $1 billion dollars and they started doing all sorts of construction work. There was a trade school in Detroit which was supported by the billion. I took classes there, they were cheap, and I learned carpentry, drywall and plastering. Then I got a job on Belle Isle doing that stuff and started making some real good money. I got off the government programs, still saved money and then bid on some of the work under my own name. I started my company 'Doakes and Company.' Man, I can't tell you how proud I was when I got my business cards and letterhead back from the printer, seeing my name on it. I was a somebody finally. What a feeling.

"I got more and more work, then became a general contractor, not just a carpenter and finisher, and started doing the whole building. Now I think I've built almost 1,500 homes or condos on Belle Isle. And----- 'Doakes and Company' is now 'Doakes and Sons'." Calvin gave Claudio a one armed hug and grinned. Claudio looked embarrassed.

Darin interjected, "And Sons, so Claudio, do you have a brother in the business?"

"Not yet, I have a younger brother in school still getting his business degree, but I guess he knows there's a spot for him if he wants it."

"That's a great story guys. So Belle Isle has really helped you. Started a business, turned into a family business," Joe observed.

Calvin answered, "It's not just the Doakes family. There were so many construction jobs created, it was just unbelievable. At the peak, there were 20,000 workers on Belle Isle doing construction. We had regularly scheduled buses from all over Detroit that were running directly onto the island to move Detroiters to the construction. These buses were set up only for the workers, there were so many of them. Now we don't take buses onto the island, as Belle Isle doesn't allow them as they did in the construction boom period. We take the ferry. But during the heyday, it was crazy. A lot of my friends made a lot of money doing construction and many started their own businesses.

"Yes, Belle Isle is largely getting built out. But the second boom is in Detroit. Now most of my business is in Jefferson across the bridge. I built 22 homes there just last month."

Darin glanced at his watch and said, "Calvin and Claudio, thanks for sharing your story with us, but Joe and I have a dinner reservation we have to get to. You guys take care."

They shook hands and Joe and Darin walked another block east to the restaurant.

# CHAPTER 32

*First they ignore you, then they laugh at you, then they
fight you, then you win.*

*-Mahatma Gandhi*

## THE LAST SUPPER

They resumed their discussion over the soup.

"So you were talking about capitalism and cronyism," Joe
reminded Darin.

"Yes. My point is that a society that doesn't respect individual freedom, that holds an elitist view that the common man can't make good decisions in the face of expert
opinions, that the experts must make laws to protect the
common man from his poor decisions, becomes a society
that is easily manipulated by the clever among us to their
own advantage. The few manipulators become very rich
and we who are manipulated become a little poorer. But
with each occurrence, the cumulative effect is we become
quite poor, or at least never become as wealthy as we
otherwise could.

"The manipulators are very canny. You've heard a picture is worth a thousand words. Well, an anecdote is
worth a thousand statistics. How many bad laws have
been passed because of one person's tragedy? Just look
at the laws in the U.S. that have been passed with someone's name attached to it. The politicians say look at the
polls — the majority wanted it. But majority rule, by its

very nature, stops innovation and experimentation. Majority rule is status quo. And the longer the tenure of the status quo, the tougher it is to make a substantial change. F.A. Hayek, the Austrian economist who we have named one of our streets after, said it well, 'It is always from a minority acting in ways different from what the majority would prescribe that the majority in the end learns to do better.' "

Joe asked, "So do you think what you are doing here in Belle Isle will serve as an example for others in the U.S. or the world?"

"I think some of the aspects of this society have been adopted. There is no doubt Detroit and its neighbor cities have greatly benefited by our example. Many say that is why Detroit has roared back. Whether others will pick up and follow our lead, it's hard to say; I guess time will tell. But we are basing what we do on a few core principles, which I believe are universal truths that many cultures can use," Darin replied.

"Like what?"

Darin considered his answer, "Number one — keep it simple. Not because people are stupid, they're not. It's just because when you have a lot of complexity, such as a 2,000 page piece of legislation, society needs experts to tell the common man what it means and the experts, once in the game, magically transform into elitists. And the simple principles of accountability and responsibility are thrown to the winds. Number two — if you have a dog in the hunt, go to the sidelines."

"What the heck does that mean?" Joe asked.

"It means if you're in government and your vote has some positive outcome for you personally, then recuse yourself. For example, you shouldn't be allowed to vote on your salary or whether your job should be continued. You shouldn't be allowed to vote to help some industry that contributes money to your campaign. You shouldn't be allowed to vote on public union issues when the unions are backing you financially. These are or were issues in the U.S. There are of course many more examples. We don't have those issues here."

Darin continued, "Number three — allow charity to flourish. Americans are the most generous people in the world. Belle Islanders are even more so. But government through its social programs crowds out charity. People don't see the need if the function is being performed by government. They also don't have the extra money to give to charity if it's been already taken by taxes. That's where we have really excelled here on the island. People who are taxed against their will and the money given to others without the giver's input feel a lot of resentment about the process and in many cases the recipient. But those who are given the opportunity to freely give feel good about themselves and feel positive toward those who are the beneficiaries. It's a win/win. One of my favorite sayings regarding taxes and charity is 'at least they could ask!'

"Number four — everyone needs to have skin in the game. All citizens, unless they are truly unable through no fault of their own, such as the mentally deficient or grossly disabled, need to pay something toward what they receive. People do not value that which is given to them. They do value and take care of things they either own or items they paid for. Take education as an example. Who studies harder on the average — the kid who puts himself through school with his own money earned by summer jobs, or the kid whose parents have picked up the whole bill?"

Darin continued, "Number five — don't spend more than you take in. Seems pretty simple, doesn't it? But look at all the countries in history that didn't follow that rule, until it was too late. Even the U.S., once the richest country in the world, didn't do it where it had the resources to easily do so. The dollar isn't worth squat and Americans are generally poor, at least in our view."

Joe asked, "Is that it? Is there more?"

Darin replied, "Yeah, there is one more thing that America sometimes seems to forget, and it's the ground on which both America and Belle Isle were built.

"Freedom and opportunity excite people and seem to bring out the best in our species, and capital follows these and the competitive advantage that flows from them. This is what creates the jobs and the lives our people really want.

"Freedom and opportunity — that's it."

The main courses were served and they changed the subject to old high school and college memories. Darin always felt engaging in political discussions during dinner was bad for his digestive health.

After dessert, they walked outside.  The street lights were a combination of soft glowing electric lamps and gas lights.  The beauty of the setting gave Joe an inner peace as he and Darin strolled the two blocks to the monorail station.  It was though the buildings, with diversity of unique designs and the streetscape stood as a monument to all the best in human qualities — passion for beauty, freedom to work hard and keep the fruits of your labor, respect for others to do the same.  It had been quite an experience for him and he wasn't anxious to return to Damascus, where life wasn't bad, but it certainly lacked what was here.

At the monorail station, Darin and Joe stopped and embraced.

"My place is close by, so I'm going to say my goodbyes here," Darin said.  "You can take the monorail back to the Four Seasons.  And have a safe drive up to Petoskey tomorrow.  You'll be seeing family, right?  And when you head back to Damascus next week, I hope you take back with you some of the ideas you picked up here in Belle Isle.  You know we don't have any copyrights or pride of authorship.  Feel free to steal anything you wish!"

"I'll be sure to do that.  Maybe you should come over to Syria and work your magic there!"

"Maybe."

# Epilogue and Acknowledgments

Perhaps Darin did go to Damascus and offer his expertise to improve that city, but if there is a sequel to this novella, it will be how Darin applied his skills to help Detroit.

Throughout history, time and time again, we have seen how one person can influence a community or region, to a much greater degree than logic would dictate. In the case of Detroit, Cadillac was the first to settle the city, later followed by Woodward with his system of street design and then Henry Ford, with his innovative manufacturing systems.

The Commonwealth of Belle Isle is not a person in the sense of Cadillac, Woodward or Ford. But it can provide the "change agency" that is so desperately needed for Detroit at this point in its history. I know the reader is probably thinking "good luck getting this done." But don't underestimate the power of an idea. The Declaration of Independence and its sentiment, "We hold these truths to be self evident, that all men are created equal, that they are endowed by their Creator with certain unalienable rights, that among these are Life, Liberty and the pursuit of Happiness," inspired a rag-tag army of 5,000 rebels to defeat the most powerful nation of its time. As mentioned in the Introduction, Mahatma Gandhi did the same thing without firing a shot. He brought down colonialism with the power of the idea that we all have a divine right to freedom, sovereignty and self-determination.

Detroit badly needs something to lead it out of its depression. The $1 billion would solve a lot of budget problems and could be used fruitfully for relocation expenses, as neighborhoods will need to be consolidated. The concept of Belle Isle will attract people from all over the U.S., Canada, Europe, Asia and South America who will want to live in the community, not only for its freedom and good governance, but because it is centrally located in the largest economy of the world. The influx of these people will bring Detroit back as they are not going to spend all their money or time on a 1,000 acre island. Their economic influence will extend far beyond Belle Isle.

If done right, the Four Seasons hotel will become an icon to the world, just as the Opera House has to Sydney, Australia. Photos of Detroit will always include a piece of Belle Isle showing the Four Seasons. You can count on it!

The reader may ask, "How much is fact and how much is fantasy?" For those readers not familiar with Detroit, Belle Isle is a real place and is accurately described in terms of size and location. The main characters Joe and Darin are based on real people as is Darin's brother Andrew. Hector Cabrera is based on a real person from the Baja peninsula village of Vicente Guerrero. The Troublemakers are a real group and have already made significant contributions to improving Michigan society. The Mackinac Center is a real think tank and the article "For Whom the Belle Tolls" was a real article. Although Yuri Servenkov's character is fictional, his story about the Phoenix aircraft supplier and Michigan's reputation is entirely true.

I want to thank some of the people who have contributed reviews or advice on this novella. My liberal Ann Arbor friend Doug Turner gave me sound advice, after reviewing an early draft, to make sure Belle Isle did not become a rich man's gated island. That is certainly not my intent and I hope the reader can see that.

David Littmann, former Chief Economist of Comerica Bank and currently an Adjunct Scholar with the Mackinac Center for Public Policy, spent considerable time educating me on the Scottish Free Banking System. I didn't use that concept entirely, but did adopt the principle of private bank insurance. David also suggested the Belle Isle currency be 100% backed by a basket of commodities, rather than simply one, such as gold.

Manny Lopez, formerly with the Detroit News and now Managing Editor of Michigan Capitol Confidential, provided not only editing support, but also substantive advice in the philosophies and approaches of the book.

Hal Sperlich, former President of Chrysler Corporation, is the father of the Mustang, K-car and minivan, and a great visionary. Hal reviewed the manuscript and has inspired me to think positively about the possibility of actually making this happen. Hal also commented after reading an early manuscript that Belle Isle is all about "unlimited opportunity." So I have incorporated that label many times in the final copy. I also want to thank Hal for putting his enthusiasm for the book in writing by penning the Commentary section.

I hope the reader shares Hal's and my optimism. Big problems need big solutions. Nibbling on the fringes won't make it happen.

These mighty gifts — freedom, sovereignty and self-determination can be ours once again. All we need are three signatures to enable the miracle — the Mayor, the Governor and the President.

Simple really, that's all it takes — the rest will unfold from the power unleashed.

Rodney Lockwood

November, 2012

## How to Obtain More Information

The author is setting up a web-site at the address, which will be operational in January, 2013:

www.commonwealthofbelleisle.com

The web-site will contain much information about the Belle Isle concept, including current events and how to become involved. There will be a FAQ section which will answer many questions, in addition to a short video on Belle Isle.

The author may be contacted at

rlockwood@commonwealthofbelleisle.com

Made in the USA
San Bernardino, CA
29 July 2013